"Ah, so you'r

The voice to her left made her start. Abby felt a surge of fear, but in light of the yellow curtains, white walls and the very pregnant woman staring down at her, she managed to swallow that fear and ask, "What happened? Where am I?"

"You're in my home. I'm Fiona Whitley. My mom and my brother, Cal, rescued you when you passed out at the bus station."

Abby sat up and regretted the quick action when the room spun. "When was that?"

"Three days ago. Today's Friday. Your fever finally broke yesterday."

Abby remembered her self-diagnosis in the bus station. And with that memory came the vision of the man who'd been following her. "Oh, no," she whispered.

"What's wrong?"

Did she dare burden her? Abby looked around the cozy apartment and realized she couldn't just blurt out she thought someone was following her. A person who had evil intentions toward her....

Books by Lynette Eason

Love Inspired Suspense

Lethal Deception
River of Secrets
Holiday Illusion
A Silent Terror
A Silent Fury
A Silent Pursuit
Protective Custody
Missing
Threat of Exposure
*Agent Undercover
*Holiday Hideout

*Rose Mountain Refuge

LYNETTE EASON

grew up in Greenville, South Carolina. Her home church, Northgate Baptist, had a tremendous influence on her during her early years. She credits Christian parents and dedicated Sunday school teachers for her acceptance of Christ at the tender age of eight. Even as a young girl, she knew she wanted her life to reflect the love of Jesus.

Lynette attended the University of South Carolina in Co-lumbia, South Carolina, then moved to Spartanburg, South Carolina, to attend Converse College, where she obtained her master's degree in education. During that time, she met the boy next door, Jack Eason, and married him. Jack is the executive director of the Sound of Light Ministries. Lynette and Jack have two precious children—Lauryn and Will. She and Jack are members of New Life Baptist Fellowship Church in Boiling Springs, South Carolina, where Jack serves as the worship leader and Lynette teaches Sunday school to the four- and five-year-olds.

Holiday Hideout

LYNETTE EASON

Love Inspired

Recycling programs
for this product may
not exist in your area.

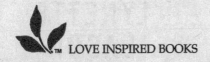

™ LOVE INSPIRED BOOKS

ISBN-13: 978-0-373-44470-0

HOLIDAY HIDEOUT

Copyright © 2011 by Lynette Eason

www.LoveInspiredBooks.com

Printed in U.S.A.

You are my hiding place; you will protect me from trouble and surround me with songs of deliverance.
—*Psalms* 32:7

To my family, I love you all.

ONE

Dr. Abigail O'Sullivan stepped off the bus and felt the hair on the back of her neck spike. It was all she could do to hold back the groan climbing up her throat as she looked around, trying to pin down the source of her uneasiness.

It's nothing, she told herself, *you were careful. There's no way he could have followed you. You're just sick.*

The fever had started yesterday. Monday, right? She thought so. The aches and pains had followed shortly thereafter. She needed something to drink. Some water. But she'd been on a bus for the past three hours fading in and out. During a lucid moment, she wondered exactly how high her fever was.

But was it truly just illness causing her to feel so out of sorts?

Even now, exhausted and sick, she felt watched. *How?* her sluggish mind cried. She'd taken buses, crisscrossed states, paid cash for everything. Her dry eyes burned as they canvassed the area around her. How could he still be behind her?

He's not, he couldn't be.

His parting words made her shudder. "I'm going to make sure you suffer for the rest of your life."

Cutting words. Hurtful, hateful words.

But that's all she'd thought they were.

Just words.

Until someone tried to run her off the road and the police blamed her and chalked it up to reckless driving.

And then there was the series of incidents that frightened her terribly. Coming home to find her house had been searched was terrifying. Then her car had been broken into and her office searched.

Subtly. Very carefully. But she'd known it. And she'd reported it to the police.

Who'd done absolutely nothing.

She snorted. The police. A lot of help they were.

So was it him? Or someone else? Possibly someone he'd hired? A chill shook her, and she pulled the edges of her coat tighter. Her tongue snaked out to lick dry lips. Snagging her purse, she rummaged through it until she found a crumpled bill and some change. Surely there'd be a drink machine somewhere in this bus station.

Her mind hopped back to the person after her.

If he'd hired someone, then she'd have to keep running no matter how awful she felt. Swallowing hard, she grimaced at the pain the action brought. She felt sure gulping razors wouldn't hurt as much. Vaguely, she wondered if she had strep in addition to the flu.

Probably. She thought about the young boy on the last bus. He'd been coughing, flushed and complaining his throat hurt. Abby had wondered if he had the flu or strep.

Now she knew.

"Are you all right, dear?"

Abby turned to look at the woman who'd posed the question in a light Irish accent and had to fight off a wave of dizziness. When her head stopped spinning, she took note of stylish salt-and-pepper hair before landing on the green eyes glistening with concern. Abby guessed the lady was in her mid-fifties.

Feeling a cough coming on, Abby turned her face into her elbow until the spasm passed. Using the tissue she'd found in the bottom of her purse, she dabbed the cough-induced tears from under her eyes. "I'm sorry. I'm just sick. The flu, I think, and maybe strep, too, so you might want to keep your distance."

But the gentle lady smiled. "I've had my shot. And I've never had strep in my life. Guess I'll take my chances. I'm waiting on my son to pick me up. Been visiting my sister over in Bryson City."

Dizziness swept over Abby again and she closed her eyes to ward it off. She didn't bother telling the woman she'd had her flu shot, too. Fat lot of good it had done her.

When she opened her eyes, her new friend placed a hand on her arm and led her to a nearby bench. "But you don't care about all that. Here, why don't you sit here while I get you a bottle of water?"

Before Abby could protest, another wave of dizziness attacked her and she sank onto the bench with a grateful groan.

A shiver racked her and she huddled deeper into her thick down winter coat. The middle of December in North Carolina was *cold*. Of course the fever didn't help. Squinting, she fought sleep even though she wanted nothing more than to curl up and sink into oblivion.

Unfortunately, she couldn't do that. She had to stay

awake, keep her eyes peeled. Stay alert. *He* would be waiting for her to show weakness, catch her off guard.

But she'd been so *careful*.

She reached down and patted the small bulge in the lower part of her jeans. The reassuring feel of the wad of cash soothed some of her anxiety.

She looked around again and another tremor shook her as the faces blended, merged, then separated. Abby blinked fast to clear her vision.

Yes, she'd been careful.

At least she thought she had. But what if she hadn't been? What if her paranoia wasn't fever-induced? After all, what did she know about running from someone who caught criminals for a living? Not that she was a criminal, but the process was the same wasn't it?

Visions of her brother-in-law's stony glare as Abby clutched her dead sister's hand stumbled to the forefront of her brain.

Her sister and baby girl…dead because of Abby…

Grief racked her. "My fault."

"Here, darling. Here's your water."

Abby felt liquid slip between her lips to cool her fiery throat. "Thanks," she whispered.

"What's your name?"

"Abby."

"Well, Abby, I'm Justine McIvers and I think we need to get you to a doctor. Are you meeting someone here?"

"No, I'm alone. But I'll be all right." The water did seemed to revive her a bit. She took another swallow and nearly cried at the pain the action caused.

Then her eyes fell on a man behind the woman and she gasped, shoved aside the water and lurched to her feet. She stumbled, got her balance, then fell headlong into a hard chest.

Strong hands grasped her upper arms. "Whoa, there, little lady. What's going on?" The deep bass voice rumbled in her ear.

"She's very sick, Cal," the woman behind her said. "I think she needs an ambulance."

"No, please," Abby gasped. "No, no ambulance, no hospitals."

The darkness started closing in and she fought it. She couldn't pass out! Not now. He was here! He'd found her. She looked again and didn't see him.

Or was he just a hallucination?

Panicked, she looked up into the blue eyes of the man who kept her from landing face-first on the floor at his feet. "Don't let him get me."

And then she lost the battle as blackness coated her.

Deputy Sheriff Callum McIvers held the sick woman against him, his eyes scanning the gawking crowd. Who was she afraid of?

Don't let him get me. Her words echoed in his ears.

Who? In a town the size of Rose Mountain, Cal prided himself on knowing just about every resident by name.

Except during the holiday season. Christmas was right around the corner, and every day the bus brought more strangers to town than he could count.

Even through both of their heavy winter coats, he could feel the heat from the fever emanating from the woman who'd just passed out.

Trained as a first responder, he acted quickly. Doing a preliminary check, he was relieved to find a strong pulse. However, her breathing seemed labored. Probably from the congestion in her chest.

Cal looked up at his mother, whose concern was

etched on her normally smooth forehead. He said, "We need to get her to a doctor. She's burning up."

"She said it was the flu and possibly strep."

Cal frowned. "Call Dylan and have him meet me at the house. She's obviously afraid of someone, so I guess I won't take her to the hospital if she doesn't need to go. If she's running from someone, her illness could be a combination of exhaustion and whatever bug she's picked up."

"You're taking her home? To your house?" Surprise lit his mother's eyes as Cal picked the woman up in his arms and ignored the crowd that had gathered to watch the drama play out.

"Well, maybe not to my house. Yours isn't a very good idea with you promising to watch Tiffany this week. We sure don't want her to come down with whatever this woman's got." Tiffany was the five-year-old granddaughter of his foreman, Zane Dodson. Zane's daughter, a single mother and a doctor, had volunteered to go to Haiti for a week on a mission trip. Zane was excited about having the little girl nearby, but the thought of caring for her by himself had terrified him. Cal's mother had stepped in and volunteered to help babysit.

Cal said, "What about Fiona's? I don't want to expose Fiona to her, though. What do you think?"

"If we take her to Fiona's, she can have the apartment in the basement. I can come over and check on her, bring her food or whatever until she's past the contagious stage."

Cal nodded. "Sounds like a plan. I've got the car outside. Do you have Dylan's number?"

"Sure. And I've got her purse, too. Let's go."

Cal carried her out, doing his best to shield her from the cold wind blowing off the mountain.

As he settled the unconscious woman into the backseat, his mother climbed in the front. "Dylan said to bring her by his office, it's quicker. He's already shut down for the day and happened to be there working on some files. He can see her right away."

"Excellent."

Once more, Cal checked her pulse. Still strong.

"I don't know if she had a bag other than her purse or not."

Cal grunted as he worked the seat belt around her. "I'll call Joe and tell him to hold it if a strange bag shows up with no one to claim it."

Joe was the bus transit director and one of Cal's good friends.

Cal climbed into the front seat and started the engine. Five minutes later, he pulled into the parking lot of Dylan Seabrook's medical practice. A quick scan of the road behind him showed no cars, no one following. But the fear on the woman's face just before she passed out stayed with him.

Gathering the sick woman in his arms, he headed for the door. Dylan swung it open. "I was watching for you. Bring her on down here."

Cal followed Dylan down the hall to an empty room. As gently as possible, he settled her on the examination table and looked at Dylan. "We'll be right outside."

Dylan took over as Cal took his mother's hand and pulled her from the room.

His mother spoke. "What makes you think she's afraid of someone?"

"She said, 'Don't let him get me,' just before she passed out."

She blanched. "Oh, my."

Cal nodded. "Did you see anyone suspicious hanging around her?"

"No, darling, I was just looking for you and noticed how flushed she was. She also looked a little lost, so I asked her if she needed some help."

Cal smiled. "Leave it to God to lead you to the one who needs help." He glanced at the door wondering what was taking so long. How sick was she? He started to get concerned. Had he misjudged the seriousness of her illness?

Outside the window at the end of the hall, darkness had fallen and the full moon cast shadows.

His gaze sharpened. Wait. Was that someone trying to look in? "I'll be right back."

"What is it?" She frowned up at him.

"Just want to check something out, all right?"

"Cal, you've got that look on your face."

But he was already moving toward the front door. He could feel her worried gaze drilling his back as he turned the corner.

Once outside, he stopped and listened. Had he just imagined the shadow outside the window?

Making his way as silently as possible around to the back of the building, he found the window where he thought he'd seen the image of someone trying to peer inside the building.

Nothing stirred but the normal end-of-day noises and his breath in the air.

A footfall to his left.

Cal whirled. The shadow ran.

"Hey! Freeze! Police!"

Ignoring him, the person never stopped. Cal took off after him, boots slapping against the asphalt as he rounded the side of the building.

Squinting, Cal tried to get a look at the fleeing man, but in the darkness, even with the light of the moon, wasn't able to make out much more detail than the man's baseball cap. He thought the guy had on a dark colored heavy coat and boots, but wasn't a hundred-percent sure.

The figure slipped between The Candy Caper and John's General Store. Cal heard the roar of an engine, but by the time he got around the corner, man and vehicle were gone, taillights fading in the distance. In the dark behind the buildings, he couldn't even get a make on the car or a license plate.

Cal slapped his thigh in frustration as he stopped to catch his breath even as his brain started processing the events.

A sick woman—whose name he still didn't know—in a bus station. A frightened plea for help. A stranger lurking outside the medical building where the woman was receiving care.

Who was he? An ex-husband or a boyfriend?

Had Cal found himself in the middle of a domestic violence situation?

His jaw tightened as he stared in the direction of the long-gone taillights as another woman's pleas echoed in his ears. Another woman he'd failed.

If this new stranger he and his mother had taken under their wing needed help, Cal would do everything in his power to make sure she received protection and care for as long as she needed it. And from whomever she was scared of.

Dylan gave a disgusted grunt and turned to walk the three blocks back to the clinic.

When he entered the door, his mother greeted him with a worried look. "Are you all right?"

"I'm fine."

"What made you think you needed to go check on things outside?"

Not wanting her to worry, Cal shook his head. "Just a feeling. But everything's all right." He changed the subject. "How's our patient? Have you heard anything?"

"Not yet. I'm worried she might need—"

Dylan opened the door and Cal pounced. "How is she?"

"She's sick." The doctor's brow furrowed. "I suspect strep and the flu." He held up two capped tubes. "I took some cultures, so we'll know something in a few minutes after I get them processed."

Dylan walked into the lab and began the process that would read the cultures. Cal followed on his heels. "Did she wake up? Why did she faint?"

As Dylan washed his hands, he looked over his shoulder at Cal. "Yes, she woke up. I talked to her a bit, but she's not making much sense. Talking about someone being after her?" Dylan lifted a brow. "Do you have any idea what that's related to?"

"I might. In the bus station she seemed scared, then before she passed out she said, 'Don't let him get me.'"

Dylan frowned. "That doesn't sound so good."

"Exactly." He hardened his jaw.

His friend gave him a knowing look. He knew exactly what Cal meant. "Well, I gave her something for the fever, so it's coming down. She's worn out and pretty dehydrated. As for your second question as to why she fainted, I think that was probably due to a combination of things."

"So, does she need to be in a hospital?"

"Nah." Dylan dried his hands on the towel. "Like I said, she's a little dehydrated, but if someone will make sure she gets proper rest and care, she'll be good as new in a few days. I can even come out there in a couple of days to check her over."

Cal thought about the man he'd just chased. If he was after the sick woman, he was going to have to go through Cal to get to her.

And Cal wasn't an easy man to go through.

TWO

Abby blinked at the sunlight streaming in through the window to her left. Awareness came to her slowly, almost as though she were slogging through a fog. Her eyes were immediately drawn to the opposite wall where a collection of weapons hung on display.

Knives, guns, rifles, a slingshot?

And a Christmas tree on a small table in the corner of the room. Multicolored lights twinkled in a repeating pattern.

Where in the world was she?

Turning her head, she squinted to take in the rest of her surroundings.

"Ah, so you're awake now?"

The voice with the soft Irish accent made her start. The smell of chicken broth made her stomach rumble. Abby felt a surge of fear, but in light of the yellow curtains, cream-colored walls and the very pregnant woman staring down at her, she managed to swallow that fear and ask, "What happened? Where am I?"

Bits and pieces of the past few days flitted through her mind. A woman helping her to the bathroom. A cool cloth placed on her forehead. Sipping some broth. A shot? Yes, she definitely remembered the shot.

She looked at the woman in front of her and decided she looked familiar, but she wasn't the one she'd seen in her dreams.

Or was it all real?

"I'm Fiona Whitley. You're in my home in our small basement apartment. My mom and my brother, Cal, rescued you when you passed out at the bus station."

"Passed out!" Abby sat up and regretted the quick action when the room spun. Closing her eyes, she waited. When she opened them, things had settled, but she still felt as weak as a newborn. "When was that?"

"On Tuesday. Today's Friday. Your fever finally broke yesterday. You've had a nasty case of the flu and strep throat. Dr. Seabrook came by and gave you some fluids by IV. After that, you seemed to start improving hourly."

Abby remembered her self-diagnosis in the bus station. And with that memory came the vision of the man who'd been following her. "Oh, no," she whispered.

The pretty woman with the red curls and green eyes frowned. "What's wrong?"

Did she dare burden her? Abby looked around the cozy apartment and realized she couldn't just blurt out she thought someone was following her.

A person who had evil intentions toward her. "Has… um…anyone been looking for me? Asking about me?"

"Not that I know of." Fiona gave her a wry smile. "We live on a large ranch, not exactly a hub of excitement and information. Fortunately, we have all of the modern conveniences. Do you have someone you'd like me to call?"

"No!" At Fiona's start, Abby softened her tone. "No. No one."

"But surely someone's missed you by now." Fiona sat

on the bed beside Abby. "We found your phone in your purse, but the battery's missing."

"I took it out." She remembered thinking that somehow her whereabouts could be traced through the phone's location, so she'd pulled the battery out and sewn it and her driver's license—and the flash drive—into the leg of a pair of her jeans. An extreme measure maybe, but she just wanted to disappear. She didn't want to be Abby O'Sullivan for as long as it took to find a slice of peace and put her life back together.

A guilty look flashed across Fiona's face. "We went through your things trying to find out who you are."

"My things?" At first she was alarmed, then calmed. She hadn't had very much. "That's all right." They wouldn't have found her identification. A fact that was probably weighing on the pretty woman's mind. Abby said, "I'm Abby. Abby…um…Harris." She picked at the comforter as she gathered her strength. "Thanks so much for taking care of me." Her eyes landed on the woman's belly. "I sure hope you don't get sick."

"Mom didn't want me near you, either," Fiona admitted with a small laugh. "She used to be a nurse and insisted on doing most of the caring for you. And Dylan came by a couple of times." Fiona smiled. "So no worries, I'm fine and so is the little one."

Abby swung her legs to the side of the bed and realized she had on a pair of strange pajamas. "Where did these come from?"

Fiona gave another light giggle. "They're mine. I outgrew them quite a while ago—" she patted her distended belly with a loving hand "—but they looked like they might fit you." She bit her lip. "I hope you don't mind, but we couldn't leave you in your clothes once your fever broke now, could we? Mom helped me get you into those."

"No, I guess not." She'd had pajamas in her bag.

As though reading her thoughts, Fiona offered, "We didn't get your bag from the bus station until yesterday afternoon."

That explained it. Abby pulled in a deep breath. "I really appreciate you all taking care of me. It was a very kind thing to do."

Fiona smiled and something flashed in her eyes. Something Abby wanted to discern but couldn't quite put her finger on. She ignored it and said, "I probably should get going."

She tried to stand and another wave of dizziness almost knocked her down.

Fiona took her by the arm and helped her lie back down on the bed. "You aren't going anywhere until you get better. You're welcome to stay here until you feel well enough to leave."

Abby wanted to argue but couldn't summon the energy. She knew Fiona was right. But the problem was, she had someone after her.

The other problem was she didn't have the strength to do anything about it. She lay on the bed and closed her eyes for a moment, trying to take everything in that had happened in the past several months.

Would Reese really go this far? Was he still after her? Or had the fever caused her to hallucinate in the bus station?

Even though he fully believed—as did she—that the deaths of his wife and her baby were her fault, would he really go to the extreme of following her this far?

She honestly didn't know, but it sure looked like it.

But why would he search her apartment? Why would he try to get in her window in the middle of the night?

To keep her off balance? To make her so afraid of her own shadow that when he finally pounced, she'd be an easy target?

Possibly.

"What do you think?"

Fiona's question made Abby blink. She realized she hadn't heard a word the woman said. "I'm sorry. I was thinking… What'd you say?"

"I said I think it might be a good idea for you to stay here awhile. Unless you have someone—"

"No. Like I said, there's no one." No one at all. Her family had disowned her the minute her sister had taken her last breath.

Because it was her fault her sister had died. At least that's how she felt. And so did her family.

Shuddering, she looked at Fiona, grief piercing her as she studied the large bulge under the woman's blue maternity shirt. "When is your baby due?"

An excited smile curved Fiona's lips. "Right after the first of the year. My due date's January 2."

"That's wonderful for you. Just about three more weeks, eh?"

"Yes." The word was more of a groan. "And it can't come soon enough."

As an obstetrician, Abby figured if she had a dollar for each time she'd heard those words from an expectant mother, she'd be a millionaire.

"I don't—"

A knock on the door jarred her to a stop. Heart in her throat, she grabbed the blanket and pulled it to her chin. Like it could protect her from whoever was on the other side of that door.

Compassionate green eyes watched her, saw her fear. "It's all right," Fiona said. "It's probably my mother or my brother, Cal. My husband sold two of our horses and went to deliver them to a family in Virginia. He'll be home Monday afternoon."

Feeling like an idiot, Abby relaxed her death grip on the blanket and nodded. Of course it couldn't be Reese. If it was, he certainly wouldn't announce his presence with a knock.

Fiona opened the door and a tall man with reddish-blond hair and blue eyes deep enough to swim in stepped over the threshold.

The man from the bus station.

The man whose strong arms had easily caught her when she'd dropped like a felled deer.

Abby couldn't help the flush on her cheeks because, while he didn't know this, she was embarrassed that she could remember what his arms felt like around her.

And flustered because she wished she could fall into the comfort of them once more.

How long had it been since she'd had someone hold her and offer—

She blinked the thought away. Right now she had to concentrate on getting well and leaving before she brought trouble to this sweet family.

Only then did his uniform register.

The gray shirt, black pants, black tie. And the gold badge placed just over his heart.

He was a cop.

Her heart thudded. She gulped and looked away.

"Hi, there, how are you feeling?"

His deep voice sent shivers all over her. Shivers that had nothing to do with a fever she no longer had. "Hi. Better, thanks."

Fiona said, "This is Abby Harris. Abby, this is my brother, Callum McIvers."

Cal smiled, revealing even white teeth. And twin dimples on his clean-shaven face. "But you can call me Cal. All my friends do. Nice to meet you, Ms. Abby Harris. A beautiful name for a beautiful girl."

He was charming. Oh, my. Abby felt she might need to grab ahold of her heart with both hands before it ruptured from her chest. First he'd rescued her, now he flattered her. "I hear I owe you a thank you."

"Well, I never could resist a woman falling at my feet." He winked.

Her flush burned hotter.

Fiona slapped Cal's arm. "Stop it."

Cal laughed and cowered from his sister in mock fear. Abby watched their exchange and felt grief pierce her heart. She and Keira used to joke around like that.

"So, Ms. Harris." His voice turned serious. "What are you doing here in Rose Mountain?"

Pulling in a deep breath, Abby ignored the flash of guilt at using a fake name and shrugged. Hoping she came across as nonchalant, she was seriously afraid she failed. "First of all, please call me Abby. And I…um… well, I decided to take a…vacation. Unfortunately, it looks like I took a little detour instead."

"Where are you headed?"

Anywhere that took her away from the man after her. "Nowhere specific. I was just going to find a spot that looked nice and quiet and rent a little cabin. Have some time to myself."

"So you have no reservations somewhere?" His right brow lifted like he had trouble believing her.

Abby sighed and told the truth—at least part of it. "Look, I've been working very hard. There's no mystery here. I decided to take some time off. So I got on a bus that was going in the direction I wanted to go. I'd been traveling for about four days, sightseeing, enjoying the mountains and all that touristy stuff, before I took that header in the bus station."

"Four days?" Fiona looked shocked.

Abby forced a little laugh. "I know. It sounds crazy, doesn't it?" Not too crazy, she hoped. After all, it was almost the complete truth. She *had* decided to stop and find a cabin. She just hadn't planned on it taking her quite so long to lose her brother-in-law. At least that's who she thought was following her.

Come to think of it, she hadn't gotten a very good look at the man.

However, the man in the bus station definitely looked like Reese. That is, if she hadn't been hallucinating. And if she hadn't been hallucinating, then all of her evasive tactics had failed.

Cal settled himself in the chair in the corner and she felt his astute gaze on her. It made her want to squirm. He asked, "Do you remember what you said to me right before you passed out?"

Her mind raced. What had she said? "No, sorry, I don't remember."

He steepled his fingers under his chin. "You said, 'Don't let him get me.'"

Abby flinched. "Are you sure I said that?"

"I'm sure."

Abby bit her lip and looked away. How should she respond? How could she explain without lying and yet protect herself at the same time.

"Are you in trouble, Abby?"

"Not with the law," she blurted.

Compassion flickered in his eyes and he exchanged a

look with Fiona. She wondered what it meant. Then he asked, "Are you involved in a domestic violence situation?"

Abby blinked. Domestic violence? "Yes, he's—" She broke off and took a deep breath. "Yes, I suppose you could say that, which is why I probably need to leave. I sure don't want to repay all of your kindness by bringing trouble to your doorstep."

Cal's jaw tightened. "Trust me, if trouble shows up on this doorstep, I'll be ready for it."

Abby couldn't read the exact emotion in his eyes, but Fiona blinked fast like she was holding back tears. Wondering at the sudden tension in the room, Abby waited to see if one of them would enlighten her.

Neither did.

Well, she supposed that was only fair. She wasn't sharing all of her secrets, either.

"When you're a bit better, we'll take you into town to get checked out again by Dylan—or he can come by here," Fiona offered softly.

"Dylan?" That was the second time his name had mentioned. The doctor? She had a vague recollection of an unfamiliar doctor's office and a man asking her questions. But all she'd wanted to do was go back to sleep.

"Dr. Dylan Seabrook," Cal confirmed. "He's got a small practice at the base of the mountain. He's the one who got you on the antibiotics and flu meds."

"I don't really remember much about that." She thought about the money she'd tucked away in her little hidden pocket. "I suppose I need to pay him something."

Cal offered a soft smile. "No worries. We'll make all that right later when you're feeling better."

Abby lifted a brow. What doctor didn't want payment as soon as possible?

As though reading her mind, Cal laughed. "Welcome to Rose Mountain."

And what a welcome. Abby couldn't stop the shiver that shook her. While she felt safe for the moment, she couldn't help but wonder how long that feeling would last.

Her glance landed on the window where the darkness pressed against the pane as though trying to get in. She wondered if Reese was watching this very minute. If somehow he'd managed to follow her out to this ranch.

The thought made her sick. His words rang in her ears. "This is your fault. You'll pay for this. I'm going to make sure you suffer every day for the rest of your life."

It looked like he was well on his way to keeping his promise.

THREE

Saturday morning, Cal jammed the pitchfork into the pile of hay and tossed it into the nearest stall. In spite of the cold, sweat dripped from his forehead and he lifted an arm to swipe the liquid onto his sleeve.

Dropping the pitchfork to the floor of the barn, Cal slammed a fist into his palm, then turned to the punching bag hanging off to the side. He often worked out in the barn, letting off steam and trying to forget things that had a way of haunting him occasionally.

Like domestic violence victims.

Just the thought of someone trying to hurt Abby made his blood boil. He pounded the bag until the sweat started to drip into his eyes. Peeling off the heavy sheepskin coat, he draped it over the nearest stall and went back to pummeling until his hands throbbed.

"Boy, you better slow down or you're going to pull something."

Cal whirled to find Jesse Walker, the ranch's resident horse expert, standing in the door, hands holding the reins to Teddy Bear.

Panting, Cal wiped the sweat from his forehead with his sleeve. "Hey, Jesse, sorry. I just needed a good workout this morning."

"No problem." He paused and looked behind him. "You got company coming. I'm going to go give Teddy Bear here his own workout."

Cal nodded and Jesse left.

Something nudged his shoulder and he turned to find Snickers begging for a treat. Cal felt his blood pressure ease off at the horse's affection. Reaching up, he rubbed the stallion's silky nose. "I couldn't help Brianne, Snickers, but I can help this woman."

The horse nosed his hand and tried to nibble. Cal reached into his pocket for the apple he always brought with him. Snickers made short work of it.

"Hi."

Cal turned to see Abby standing in the door of the barn.

The company Jesse had mentioned.

She had her red curls pulled up in a ponytail. Dressed in a pair of black jeans, a black turtleneck and a cream-colored wool sweater under a heavy black coat she'd left unbuttoned, he thought she looked a hundred-percent better than she did yesterday. "Hey, what are you doing up?"

She shrugged. "I've been lying in that bed so long, I needed to get up. Fiona said you were in the barn." She smiled as she took in the horses lining the stalls. "Wow, you have a nice operation here."

"Thanks. It's a family thing. We board horses. We also breed and sell them."

Cal watched Abby wander over to Snickers and rub the horse's left ear. Snickers threw his head up, then brought it back down like he approved. Cal let his eyes take in the sight of Abby again, thinking the horse had good taste.

Planting his fists on his hips, he watched her run

her hands over Snickers, admiring the strength of the animal. "You're comfortable with horses."

She looked at him over her shoulder and nodded. "I grew up riding. Our neighbors had horses and they let me and my sister come over and ride anytime we wanted."

Cal wondered at the flicker of grief he'd seen flash in her eyes. Then it was gone, and he decided he'd imagined it.

"Well, there are plenty of places to ride out here." He pointed to his left. "In that direction, there're trees that back up to the main road. The river on this property runs right under it." He pointed right. "That way is land for about as far as you can see, but at the end of it, you can see the highway." Pride filled him as he let his gaze wander the land he called home. He loved it and wouldn't want to live anywhere else. "The three houses make a triangle. The main house, where mom lives, sits up on the hill overlooking the rest of the land. You can see the other two houses from it. My house is that way and you know where Fiona's is. We all live within a mile of each other. When you feel up to it, I'll take you for a ride over the land, show you the rest of the layout and tell you all about it."

Life filled her green eyes for the first time since he'd met her. "That would be lovely."

"We'll plan on it, then."

She smiled and he felt his heart thud an extra beat in anticipation of spending time with her. She nodded to the wall. "You collect weapons?"

He nodded. "Well, my dad did. He died from a massive heart attack last year." Grief still filled him when he thought about the man. "He was a big collector." Cal jabbed the pitchfork once more, then leaned it against the wall as he stared at the weapons. "I'm sure you noticed the wall in the little apartment."

At her nod, he said, "Those were Dad's, too. I guess one day, I'll take them down and store them, but for now..." He shrugged.

Her sympathetic look said she understood. For a moment he just stood there, staring at her, taking in her beauty, unable to look away.

"Hi, Uncle Cal." The little girl's voice grabbed his attention and he swung around to see his mother standing in the door of the barn holding Tiffany's mittened hand.

He smiled. "Well, hey there, kitten."

"I'm not a kitty," Tiffany protested with a giggle. "Who's her?" She pointed to Abby.

Abby smiled and stepped forward. "I'm Abby."

"I'm Tiffany," the little girl said. Cal shook his head. That kid would talk to anyone. It was kind of scary in this day and age. Tiffany let go of his mother's hand and walked to Snickers. "I wanna ride him."

His mother laughed. "Not today. And not him. He's too big for you."

Tiffany planted tiny fists on her hips. "I'm big, too."

Cal squatted to look her in the eye. "Give me some time and I'll take you on a ride soon, I promise. If you can do that, I'll let you feed Snickers another apple."

She screwed up her nose and squinted at him. Then shrugged. "Okay." She held out her hand.

Cal gave her the apple and helped her feed the delighted horse.

He heard his mother ask Abby, "How are you feeling, dear?"

"I'm better. A little weak, but that's to be expected. I can't thank you enough for all you've done for me."

Then she grimaced. "Speaking of feeling a little weak, I think I'd better go lie back down."

Immediately, Cal went to her and grasped her hands. "What's wrong? What hurts?"

He saw the surprise in her eyes—and a new warmth as she looked at him. "I'm all right, really. Just still trying to recover. A couple hours of sleep and I'll feel like a new person."

Relieved, Cal nodded. "All right. Come on, I'll walk you back to the apartment."

"And I'll just take Tiffany back to the house," his mother said. "She was antsy and needed a little outing. I thought the barn might be a good place to start." The barn sat about midway between Fiona's and his mother's houses.

Cal flushed as he realized he'd forgotten all about his mother and Tiffany. His mother's knowing look deepened the red he was sure was prominent on his cheeks.

As his mother led Tiffany back toward her house, Cal and Abby walked the gravel path back to Fiona's. She asked him, "How many acres do you have?"

"About three thousand."

"Wow!"

He smiled. "I know. It's a lot of land for this little town. But we all pitch in to take care of it."

"That's nice that you all live near each other and get along." Her soft voice held that wistful sadness he'd seen in her eyes earlier that made him wonder about her family and what kind of situation she was running from.

Before he could ask, hoofbeats sounded behind him. He turned to see Zane Dodson gallop up. Reining in the mare, the man tipped his cowboy hat to Abby, but focused his attention on Cal. "We got a fence down in the northwest quadrant. Fortunately, we'd already moved the horses, so we're good in that area. Just need to fix the fence and find the yahoo who cut it. I've got Donny and Mike up there working on it right now. But you might want to come check it out." The look in the man's eyes made Cal's nerves sit up and take notice. Only one kind of downed fence would put that expression on Zane's face.

"You sure it was cut?"

"Yep."

"Be right there." Cal looked at Abby. "This is Zane, my right-hand man on the ranch. Zane, this is Abby, a guest here."

"Nice to meet you, ma'am." He was polite, but Cal could tell he was itching to get back to the fence.

"Where are the rest of the horses?"

"I've got 'em corralled over in the south pasture."

"We missing any?" That would be a problem.

"Nope."

Relieved, Cal nodded. "Can you ask Jesse to saddle up Snickers for me?"

"You bet." Zane galloped off toward the barn and Cal placed a hand on Abby's back. "I'll just see you back to the apartment, then go see what's going on."

"I'll be fine," Abby reassured him. "That sounds urgent. Go ahead."

Cal looked to the barn, then back to Abby. It wouldn't take Jesse long to have the horse ready. "All right, if you're sure."

She smiled, her eyes kind, encouraging him to go. "I'm sure."

"I'll see you in a little bit."

He took off, worried what the cut fence might mean.

Trespasser? Or possible horse thief? It didn't happen often in Rose Mountain, and he was going to do his best to make sure it didn't happen to the horses he was responsible for.

To be on the safe side, he'd stop by his house and grab his rifle.

Abby entered the apartment and went straight for the bed. She was still weak and the long walk after being so sick probably hadn't been the best idea. But she'd felt smothered, claustrophobic in the small bedroom and getting out had been the best medicine she could have prescribed.

Her mind went to Cal McIvers. A tall man, compassionate, welcoming. Gorgeous blue eyes and a smile to die for.

And a cop.

She swallowed a sigh and rolled to her side as she felt sleep come over her. Thoughts of Cal would have to wait. Her body needed healing.

The baby's wail brought her upright in the bed with a gasp. She blinked and rubbed her eyes.

How long had she been asleep?

A quick glance at the clock showed she'd rested for a little over an hour. Sitting still in the middle of the bed, she listened, ears straining.

Had she been dreaming?

And yet there it was again. The faint sound of a baby's cry.

Had Fiona had her baby early?

By herself?

Swinging her legs over the side of the bed, Abby stilled her panicked thoughts and found her boots.

Pulling them on, she paused when she heard a horse's whinny outside her window.

Had Cal come back? Her heart thudded at the thought of seeing him again and she took a deep breath. The man had definitely made an impression on her. He had her interest for sure. Was it because he was incredibly good-looking or the fact that he'd caught her when she passed out? Or because he was one of a dying breed? A man who took care of his family and had compassion for strangers?

Or was it that when she was with him, she didn't think about the trouble she had on her tail?

All of the above, probably.

She walked to the door and pulled it open. Another wail rent the air and Abby felt her knees lock. Grief pierced her and she almost doubled over to stop the pain. Every time she heard a baby cry, it felt like sandpaper scraping across her heart.

A gust of cold wind buffeted her and she shivered even though she still had on the warm wool sweater from earlier. Ignoring the grief roiling inside her, she focused on the sound.

With the door open, she stood still and listened. Another rising cry came from around the corner of the house. Heart in her throat, Abby rushed toward the sound. Had someone left a baby out in this cold?

Surely not!

"Hello? Is someone there? Do you need help?"

She rounded the corner and confusion filled her. A recorder? But why?

She looked around to see who could have left it there.

Nothing. The strategically planted trees swayed in the wind. Brown leaves rustled.

A shuffling sound came from behind her.

Before she could whirl to see who was there, a hand with a sweet-smelling cloth slapped over her mouth and nose.

FOUR

Cal crested the hill and pulled his horse to a halt. He couldn't keep his mind on the ranch's problems. His sister's houseguest, Abby Harris, kept intruding.

From his position, he could see the main house, his mother's house and the home he grew up in, directly in front of him. His house that he'd built six years ago sat to the left, Fiona's to the right. Where Abby was.

His eyes narrowed on Fiona's house and he decided to check in and see if Abby was feeling any better. Telling himself it was natural to be so concerned about a strange woman and that if she were sixty-five and ugly as a goat, he'd still feel the worry gnawing on his gut, he set off at a fast clip, his horse covering the ground with long, even strides.

As he approached, movement by the side of the house caught his eye.

He saw a flash of red and thought he heard a horse's shrill whinny. Clicking to his mount, he moved closer.

What was going on? It looked like someone was fighting with Abby.

"Abby!"

Spurring his horse in the sides, he urged the animal

into a full gallop. The closer he got, the clearer the picture became.

"Hey!" Someone was definitely trying to hurt Abby and her struggles seemed to be growing weaker by the second. "Stop! Police!"

Grabbing the rifle from the scabbard on his saddle, Cal raised it and fired a shot into the air.

The horse's thundering hooves flew over the ground, eating up the space between him and the struggling duo.

Abby's attacker threw her to the ground and raced out of sight around to the other side of the house.

Soon, the man was on the back of a powerful animal, bolting across the open field, his horse going full out toward the edge of the property. Cal saw Abby lying still, her face turned away from him.

Grabbing his satellite phone, he punched in Zane's number. When the man answered, Cal ordered, "I've got a trespasser headed past Fiona's house to the edge of the property. He attacked Abby. Chase him down and bring him back here, but be careful, he might be armed."

"You got it."

Zane didn't waste any more words and hung up. A former special ops marine, Zane could take care of himself. Cal pulled his horse to a halt a few feet from Abby's still form.

Bolting from the saddle, he knelt beside her. "Abby." His hands ran over her, looking for any wounds. Nothing.

She moaned and he turned her on her back.

She shivered and her teeth began to chatter. Cal took a chance that nothing was broken and lifted her into his arms.

Spinning, he pushed open the door to her small apartment and stepped inside. Kicking the door shut behind him, he felt her start to struggle. "It's me, Abby, be still."

At his voice, she calmed.

Settling her on the bed, he took in her pale features. "Hey, what happened? Can you hear me?"

Puzzled, he looked her over again. No bruises anywhere, no blood. Then why wasn't she responding?

Finally, her eyelids lifted. "Cal?"

"Yeah. Who was that guy?"

"I…" She licked her lips. "I don't know. Think he had chloroform or something. I managed to avoid breathing most of it in. May have gotten a good whiff because I feel sluggish. Be all right in a little while."

Cal heard a knock on the door, then Fiona's voice, "Abby, are you down here?"

"She's here," he answered for her.

Fiona opened the door a crack. "Cal—oh, good, you're here. I heard a gunshot. Is everything all right?"

Cal's lips tightened at the worry on his sister's face. "Everything's fine now, but I think someone just tried to kidnap Abby."

"What?" Her worry turned to outrage. "Here? On our ranch? But how did anyone know she was here?"

Cal thought about the man he'd chased outside of Dylan's medical building. Was it possible he'd followed them home?

More than possible, he realized. It was the only reasonable explanation.

He turned to Abby. "Who is he? Who tried to kidnap you?"

She frowned. "I…I'm not sure. He grabbed me from behind. I never got a look at his face." Her eyes shut and he watched her force them back open. Fear stared out at him and his gut clenched.

Cal wondered if she was telling the truth. "I didn't, either. Even though I noticed he had dark hair, it was hard to tell his build through the heavy coat. I don't even think I'd recognize him if I passed him on the street. Abby, if someone's after you, I need to know who it is."

She turned her head. "It's no one. I can't believe…" She sighed. "As soon as I can, I'll be gone. I don't want to bring any more trouble to you or your family."

Cal took her fingers and squeezed. She didn't flinch or pull away, but she didn't look at him, either. "Abby, you're not the first person who's needed help around here. After today, your enemy just made the biggest mistake of his life."

"You don't mess with the McIvers or their friends," Fiona stated, eyes narrowed as though imagining what she'd do to the creep who'd dared step foot on her property to cause harm to one there. She looked at Cal. "Sounds like we might need to keep the rifles a little closer."

He nodded. "I'd say that for now."

Abby's gaze bounced back and forth between them and he smiled reassurance. "Don't worry. Now that we know trouble's here, we can keep an eye out for it."

Cal's phone rang and he pulled it off the clip on his side. He looked at Fiona. "It's Zane." Into the phone, he said, "Did you catch him?"

"Sorry, boss, by the time I got to where you said he was, he'd disappeared. I followed his trail for a while, then he started walking his horse in the river. Don't know if he went east or west. It looks like west, but I never caught up to him."

The river ran east to west dividing the property in half. About seventy-feet wide, it was one of the reasons Cal's great-grandfather had chosen this piece of land. An endless supply of water. And either way, as long as the man stayed in the shallow edge, he would be able to get off the property by following the river far enough.

Cal blew out a sigh. "All right, thanks for trying. Tell the boys to keep their guns handy. I don't want this snake anywhere near the houses. He attacked Abby and there's no guarantee he won't be back."

Cal heard Zane's swift indrawn breath. "We'll keep an eye out. Might even need a night lookout."

"Call a meeting. We need to discuss this and develop a plan."

"You got it. I'll be in touch."

Cal hung up and looked at the women who'd listened to the conversation. "Well, guess you heard. He got away."

Abby swallowed hard and her eyes closed again. "I'm sorry."

Cal looked at Fiona. "Let her sleep. I'm going to gather the men and we're going to cover the property. I want to make sure that guy is gone and gone for good." Fiona nodded and Cal left, his fury at Abby's attacker eating him from the inside out.

As soon as they finished the search, if they didn't find the man, he'd return to the ranch and start digging a little deeper into Abby's past. He refused to feel guilt at the thought.

If he didn't know who he was fighting, it would be a lost cause from the very beginning.

And for Abby's sake, this was one fight he was determined to win. Even if he had to enlist the help of every deputy on the force, he would keep Abby safe.

Abby heard the door open, then close. Cal had left. To track down the man who'd attacked her. She opened her eyes and squinted into the darkness.

Sitting up, she decided that other than a slight head-ache and the desire to take a long nap, she felt all right.

It was time to go to work. Before leaving home, she'd spent long hours at the office, on the computer, updating files and entering information. Some of it she'd done simply to escape her grief, keep her mind from her sister's death.

As a result, she'd come across information that she wanted to look at again. Saving it to a flash drive had seemed the best way to do that at the time. Now she just had to find a computer.

She thought of her attacker and shivered. Was it Reese? And when she thought about that, she couldn't stop her mind from going to one of the nights she'd worked late.

Her business partner, Dr. Randall Cromwell, had stopped by her office and compassionately told her to go home. She'd agreed. Only as she grabbed her stuff to walk out, she'd looked out the window.

And seen Reese leaning against his car, watching the building.

Waiting for her?

Obviously.

"Are you coming?" Randall had asked as she continued to stand and stare.

"I can't go out there. Reese is there by his car, waiting. He scares me." Her insides twisted in knots. "Look."

Randall had walked to the window. "He's just standing there." A pause. "He has something in his hand. Looks like a folder or a file folder of some sort. Why don't you just go out there and ask him what he wants? I'll come with you."

She'd sighed and shared, "He threatened me, Randall,

so I took a restraining order out on the man. There's no way I'm going to approach him."

Randall had pulled out his cell phone. "Then call the cops and tell them he's violated the restraining order."

"No," she'd all but shouted.

Her partner had slowly put the phone away. "Okay," he drew out the word and she knew he thought she was crazy.

"But will you walk me to my car?" she'd asked.

Randall and Abby had walked out of the office, her partner acting as her bodyguard until she was safely in her car. Reese had watched them, frustration stamped clearly on his face.

Abby wouldn't approach him, but he'd violated the restraining order by coming to her place of business.

He'd been ordered to stay off her property and he could come no closer than fifty yards if they happened to be in the same public place.

The encounter had scared her. Frightened her that he was becoming more bold. Then again, why wouldn't he be?

As Randall had opened the door for her and she slid into the car, she supposed she should call the police and report Reese.

Then she'd snorted in disgust. Like that would do any good. Reese was a cop. Cops stuck together.

She'd left the next day and within days found herself on the McIvers' ranch.

Slipping from the bed, she turned the light on and blinked at the sudden brightness. Her jeans lay draped over the chair in the small kitchen area. Her white turtleneck and blue sweater were neatly folded in the seat.

Grabbing her jeans, Abby felt for the pocket she'd sewn on the inside. Relief filled her when she felt the small lumps indicating the flash drive, cell phone battery, traveler's checks and her ID were still there.

Using a fingernail, she loosened the threads and soon had the items in the palm of her hand. Thank goodness Fiona hadn't washed her clothes or her battery would be toast. But then she wondered why she even bothered to keep it. As soon as she put it in the phone, Reese would somehow find out and track her.

If he hadn't already followed her.

The recent attack said not only was it a possibility, but it was also a probability.

She really should leave.

But how? And where would she go? She'd done her best to outrun and outsmart Reese Kirkpatrick, but all she'd done was wear herself out without shaking the man from her trail.

She'd have to decide what to do about that soon. Leave and take a chance on Reese catching up to her? Or stay and possibly put this sweet family in danger?

Not really a choice.

Clutching the flash drive, she went in search of Fiona. Hopefully, the woman had a computer she wouldn't mind Abby borrowing.

Abby knocked on the door at the top of the stairs. Almost immediately, she heard footsteps coming in her direction. Seconds later, the door opened. Fiona smiled. "I thought you were sleeping. Come on in. You haven't been up on this level yet. If you feel up to it, you can start coming up here for meals."

A flash of guilt hit her. "I'm so sorry. You've been bringing my meals down those steps. I'm sure that's not what you need to be doing in your condition."

Fiona gave a laugh. "It's not a big deal, I promise. The exercise is good for me. I don't go outside very much because we've got a bit of ice and I don't want to chance slipping." She nodded toward the window. "And it's snowing again."

Alarmed, Abby walked to the window and looked out. Big flakes fell in silent wonder. She looked back to the pregnant woman. "Aren't you worried you won't be able to get out? What are you going to do if that baby comes early?"

She shrugged. "We have a four-wheel drive and chains on the tires. Joseph said he'd get me to the hospital one way or another when the time came."

Relief filled Abby. The last thing she wanted to do was have another home delivery on her hands.

Then Fiona shattered her relief when she said, "Then again, if I wind up having the baby here, it's not a big deal. Mom's a nurse and has helped deliver a number of babies." A smile softened her eyes. "It might be kind of nice to have a home birth."

She wasn't worried about having the baby at home.

Lovely.

Memories assailed Abby, nearly suffocating her. Her sister's joyful cries as she called to tell Abby it was time. Abby's rush to Keira's home. Everything moved along like it was supposed to, then the baby just seemed to get stuck. She wouldn't move down the birth canal.

And then her sister's sudden, terrifying silence.

Abby shuddered. No way would she ever deliver another baby outside of a hospital.

"So, here we are in the kitchen." Fiona's bright voice sliced through her terrible memories.

"It's beautiful," she said, forcing a smile. "I love the Christmas tree in the corner and the mistletoe hanging above the door."

Fiona nodded. "I told Joseph I wanted a tree in every

room of the house. He thinks I'm crazy. Then he came up with the mistletoe. Said if I got a tree in every room, he got to have mistletoe hanging above every door."

Her twinkling eyes told Abby the woman didn't mind a bit. She imagined Joseph didn't mind the trees, either. A shaft of longing swept through her. Would she ever have a relationship in her life that lasted longer than one interrupted dinner? Most of the men she'd dated—and there hadn't been that many—didn't like the fact that when she was on call, she didn't waste any time getting to the hospital to deliver a new life into the world. If that meant leaving the dinner table, walking out of a movie or being unavailable on Saturday night, so be it.

But she wanted a man who could handle the crazy hours she sometimes worked.

Her mind flashed to Cal. Someone like Cal would understand. She was sure he put in some crazy hours himself as a cop. Then again, how much crime could there be in this little town?

Fiona ran a hand over the black-and-gold granite countertop. "This is my favorite place in the house. The kitchen. I love to cook and Joseph loves to eat, so it works out well."

Abby took another glance out the window and said a small prayer that the snow would stop. Then she grimaced. She'd given up talking to God the day her sister died. No need to start now. He hadn't listened then, He sure wouldn't listen now.

But a small part of her wanted to get over her anger at God. The other part argued that He could have saved Keira and she had every right to be angry with Him.

Fiona touched her arm. "Are you all right?"

Abby jerked. "Oh, sorry, just thinking. Yes, I'm fine."

Fiona didn't look like she believed it but nodded.

"The great room is off the kitchen through here. This is where we spend most of our time."

The big-screen flat-panel television mounted over the fireplace played a news channel but was on mute. Noting yet another Christmas tree in the corner of the massive great room, Abby moved to the oil painting on the wall. "Is this the ranch?"

A soft sad smile curved Fiona's lips. "Yes, a cousin of mine did it for me about a year ago. It's almost a perfect rendering of what the ranch looks like from a bird's-eye view."

"It's beautiful. Your cousin is very talented." She leaned forward and studied the signature. Brianne Sawls.

"Yes, she was. Thank you."

Was?

The sad smile and the use of the past tense made Abby wonder if the cousin was dead. Before she could ask, Fiona seemed to shove off her melancholy and said, "Two bedrooms are down the hall and two are upstairs. I thought we'd let you keep the apartment in the basement. It's more private and we won't bother you."

"The apartment is lovely. Everything is. I can't tell you how much I appreciate you letting me stay here."

A knock on the door sounded. Fiona excused herself and walked over to open it.

"Hi, Aunt Fiona." Abby heard Tiffany's high-pitched little girl voice.

"Hey, there, darling. Hi, Mom."

Abby followed, watching as Fiona helped the little girl off with her coat. Mrs. McIvers said, "We decided to take a walk in the snow and stop in to check on you."

"We're fine. I was just showing Abby around the house."

Fiona's mother held up a bulging bag. "Jesse went into town to stock up on some groceries and ran into Mrs. Paula. He dropped these off and said he gave him this for us to share."

Fiona laughed. "Fruit or veggies this time?"

"A little of both, I think."

Fiona took the bag while her mother hung her coat on the rack next to the door. "That's so kind of her." She looked at Abby. "Paula is in Mom's Bible study at church. She owns the fresh market in town and is always providing us with fresh fruit and vegetables."

"Nice." Abby's heart did something strange at that moment. And she realized what it was. A longing to belong to something like this. A community. A group of people who cared about one another, took care of each other—shared something as simple as a bag of fruit.

She loved her patients and the babies she delivered, but in the end, they were in and out of her life after about a year. She had a few "repeat customers," and that was nice, but…bottom line, Abby wanted more.

She had few friends because of her work schedule and because she'd quit going to church after Keira died. In the face of this family's love and caring for one another, her own loneliness was like a slap in the face.

Swallowing hard, Abby pushed aside the lump in her throat and decided she'd have to postpone the pity party. Fiona walked over to the sink and placed the food in it. She looked at her mother and little Tiffany. "You guys want to help me cut up and cook some fresh veggies?"

"I do!" Tiffany cried.

Fiona said, "Great. You're in charge of putting them in the steamer after I cut them. Deal?"

"Deal."

Abby asked Fiona, "Do you have a computer I could

use? I don't need the internet. I just need to look at something on a flash drive."

Fiona nodded. "Sure. You can use my laptop. We have wireless internet throughout the house if you want to check your email."

"No," Abby said quickly. "That's okay."

Not only was she afraid to use her cell phone, but she was afraid her brother-in-law—or one of his friends— might be monitoring her email account. He would be able to tell when she logged on and then trace her back to Fiona's. And that couldn't happen. Unless he'd already followed her, knew she was there and her caution was useless. The attack on her said that might just be the case.

Then again, maybe the person who attacked her was just some random trespasser and she'd been in the wrong place at the wrong time. On a ranch, in the mountains, several miles from the nearest town.

Right.

Possible? Maybe. Did she believe it? Not really.

Abby flashed back to the train station. Had she been hallucinating when she thought she'd seen Reese's face? Or had he truly been there?

There was no way to know at this point and she sure wasn't going to ask Deputy Sheriff Cal McIvers to find out for her.

Fiona emerged from a bedroom down the hall and gave Abby the laptop. She said, "You're welcome to stay up here. While I have some good help—" she looked at Tiffany and grinned "—I'm going to start working on supper."

Abby placed the laptop on the kitchen table.

Laughing, Fiona and Tiffany got to work while Abby stared out the window. Had she seen something? A glint from the sun off something metal? She waited to see if it would happen again. For several minutes, she listened to the others in the background and kept her eyes on the area where she'd seen the flash.

When nothing else happened, she shivered.

If it was Reese out there, she felt sure he would make another move soon.

She would just have to sleep with both eyes open and pray she could get away before he could fulfill his terrifying threat.

In the bunkhouse living area, Cal looked at the men in his employ and gave a silent thanks for their expertise and loyalty to his family. It was one of the leading reasons he'd hired them.

"I don't know who that guy was, but we need to make sure he doesn't come back. Who's willing to lose a little sleep at night? Maybe split the night shift? I'll pay you overtime, of course."

Donny nodded. "I'm in." Donny's family lived on the edge of Cal's property. "If he's causing trouble on your land, he might bring it over onto mine."

Mike shifted. "If he's out there, I'll spot him." Mike had been a homeless man his father had caught sleeping in the barn sixteen years ago. He'd offered him a job and a bed in the bunkhouse. Mike had been there ever since. And he'd adopted the McIvers family as his own.

Jesse crossed his arms across his ample waist and gave a nod. "We'll work out a schedule and have the ranch covered as much as possible. But with this many acres, you know we won't be able to be everywhere all the time."

Zane said nothing, but his eyes and ears didn't miss a detail, Cal knew.

Cal looked at Jesse. "I know. Like you said, we'll do what we can. I'll ask Eli if he'll let Joel and a couple of the other deputies patrol the roads bordering the ranch a little more heavily." Sheriff Eli Brody, a good sheriff and a great friend. He'd be willing to help as much as he could. Cal slapped his thighs. "Anything else?"

"Nope." Zane stood and jammed his hat onto his head. "I'm going to check out the area along the fence that was cut." He looked at Jesse. "Y'all let me know what the schedule is. I'll do whatever's needed."

Jesse nodded and Cal cleared his throat. Grateful didn't begin to describe how he felt about these men.

"I'm going to check on the girls."

By girls, he really meant Abby, he supposed, as he found himself outside her apartment door. He wiped his boots on the mat and knocked. When he didn't get an answer, he turned the knob. Unlocked.

He frowned and made a mental note to be sure to advise her to keep the door locked. Usually they didn't worry about that out here in the middle of almost nowhere, but after the incident with Abby being attacked, he'd feel better knowing she was locking the doors.

Cracking the door, he called, "Abby? You in here?"

No answer.

Pushing the door open a little farther, he scanned the inside are of the small apartment and confirmed Abby wasn't there. His gaze landed on her cell phone on the end table. The battery lay on top of it. The pile of cash next to the phone made his brows lift and his brain start clicking with various reasons she'd have that kind of money.

He stopped and stood there for about three seconds before making a decision. Picking up the battery, he slid it into the phone and powered up the device.

Was she having trouble with the phone?

The welcome screen came up, then her home screen. Seemed to be working fine.

Then again, what if that guy at the bus station was after her? The one she'd asked for protection from. Cal hesitated. Took a deep breath.

Then made sure the GPS tracking option was turned off. Not that the call couldn't be traced, but it would be a little harder and take a little longer for someone to get a location without the GPS feature.

Quickly, he scrolled through her contacts feeling only slightly guilty for doing so. But they'd—*he'd*—brought a stranger home and she was now living in his sister's house. No one would blame him for the precaution.

You could just ask her.

No, he'd already read her body language. She was hiding something. His mind went to Fiona and the baby she carried. She and Joseph trusted his judgment and were willing to open their home to Abby because Cal asked them to.

He continued to scroll.

Mom.

So she did have someone who might be worried about her.

Before he could consider the consequences of his actions, he dialed the number.

It rang twice.

"Hello?"

"Hi, is this Abby Harris's mother?"

"Harris? No. I know an Abigail O'Sullivan, though, and this is her cell phone number. Who are you and why are you calling from her phone?" The starched tone pushed his wary button.

"I'm a friend of Abby's." O'Sullivan? So, she'd used

a fake name. "She's been very sick. I thought someone might have missed her by now."

Silence. Then the woman said, "She's on vacation. At least that's what her note said. As for being sick, I'm sure she can take care of herself. Now, if that's all, I have an appointment in twenty minutes."

Incredulous at the coldhearted response, Cal asked, "Ma'am, don't you want to know where your daughter is?"

A pause. "I no longer have any daughters thanks to Abigail. So no, I'm not interested in her whereabouts."

Click.

Cal shivered and it wasn't because the room was cold. Whew. That woman sounded like she could spit icicles. If that was Abby's mother, Abby definitely had his sympathies.

He went back to the contacts. A few names and numbers that meant nothing to him.

Thinking about the revealing conversation with Abby's mother made him frown. He removed the battery once again and replaced the phone just like he'd found it.

Abby O'Sullivan.

Estranged from her family, followed and attacked by an unknown assailant. His eyes landed on the end table again. And a large amount of cash.

Just who had he brought into his family's home?

FIVE

Abby scrolled through the medical pages in front of her. After her sister's and niece's deaths, she'd thrown herself into work. Staying late, entering information usually left to the administrative staff. Doing anything to keep from going home to be alone.

The other doctors had thought she was crazy. They'd seen her fatigue and grief. Offered unwanted and unhelpful advice about taking time off. They didn't understand work was the only thing keeping her sane.

Long days of seeing patients and staying late at the office morphed into endless nights of crying and wondering what she could have done to save Keira and the baby.

Nothing, she reminded herself forcefully. Nothing. It wasn't her fault. She'd yet to see an autopsy report, didn't know if she'd be able to handle reading it when it came out. And so the guilt remained.

You did nothing *wrong,* she argued with herself.

"Yeah, well, tell that to Reese," she muttered out loud.

"Talking to yourself?" Cal asked.

Abby shrieked and spun, hand over the heart that

threatened to rupture in her chest. "Oh, my, you scared me to death."

The dimple in his left cheek appeared, and she stared at it. At him. Mesmerized by his presence. A strong compassionate man with eyes that made her melt and arms that could offer strength if she wanted to lean into them. Oh, she wanted to, she just wouldn't.

Couldn't.

He said, "I just came over to see if you were feeling any better."

"Much, thanks." She admired his handsome face. A face that said he was glad to see her. "Did you find anything about the man who tried to hurt me?"

His dimpled smile disappeared into a frown. "No. Sorry. He got away pretty fast." He rubbed his chin and looked thoughtful. "I don't think this was random, Abby. I think this guy has scoped the property, that he's been watching things going on around here."

Abby gulped. "Why do you say that?"

"Because he had it all planned out. He knew which house you were staying in and where to find you. He had the chloroform ready and he had his escape route down. This wasn't a spur-of-the-moment attack."

Fear speared her. Cal was right. It sounded like something Reese *could* do. Just not something he *would* do. Disbelief warred within her. But she knew Reese was an avid outdoorsman and he would have the equipment needed to stay out in the freezing weather. To watch, wait and make his move. She shivered and pressed a hand to her stomach that suddenly hurt.

And she couldn't think of anyone else she'd made mad enough to want to hurt her.

"So what do I do?" She stood and started to pace. "I have to leave. I can't let him come back here. If he does, he might decide to get really ugly and hurt anyone who crosses his path."

Hysteria was welling up and threatening to burst through.

Then she felt his hands on her shoulders, pulling her to him. She froze and then let herself lean on him, taking in his scent, a mixture of outdoors and spicy cologne.

For a moment, she allowed herself to feel safe. When she lifted her eyes to his, she gulped to find her lips only a fraction from his.

Her heart thudded, her stomach flipped.

And then he gently set her from him and looked over her shoulder toward the computer. "What are you working on?"

Abby licked her lips, surprised at the disappointment racing through her. She'd wanted him to kiss her.

Focusing on his question, she seriously thought about dumping the whole mess on him. And then forced herself to keep those words buried deep. He was a cop. And she wasn't fond of cops right now. Even one she wanted to kiss. She liked Cal, trusted him to keep her safe. For now. But if he found out she was running from a cop… where would his loyalties fall, then?

Instead of spilling her troubles, she said, "I was going on vacation, but I'm not one to leave work completely behind. I'm just working on some files that need updating."

She clicked the screen closed, her tongue burning with the lie. But it wasn't completely a lie. They were files from work and some of them did need updating. But for some reason, she didn't want to tell him exactly what she did for a living. That information might lead him to ask more questions, to dig deeper. And she wasn't ready to venture into that territory right now.

"Well, don't let me interrupt." His clean scent invaded her senses once again as he leaned in closer.

Looking up at him, she felt dwarfed by his towering height. As though sensing her feelings, he backed up a step.

"I have an extra laptop at home you can use if you need one throughout the day."

His generous offer surprised her. "That would be wonderful." She paused and bit her lip.

"What?" he asked reaching out his forefinger to release her bottom lip from her teeth.

The zing up her spine held her motionless for a moment. Her lip burned from his touch. Swallowing, she asked, "Why are you doing this?"

"Why not?"

Abby gave a small laugh. "Come on, Cal, in this day and age, people just don't help each other anymore. Not like this. Taking in a sick woman, letting me stay here, offering the use of a spare computer." She frowned, truly puzzled. "How do you know I won't rob you blind? Or worse?"

Those cinnamon-colored eyes crinkled at the corners. "I don't, which is why I'm keeping an eye on you." The smile softened his words, but she could tell he was serious, too.

And he should be, but Abby didn't know whether to laugh or be mad. "So why not take me to the nearest hotel and be done with me?"

He took his sweet time answering as he studied her. She shifted, uncomfortable with his probing stare. Then he smiled again, this time causing that dimple to wink at her. "Look, you were in bad shape and needed help. God seems to lead Mom to those people—or those people to Mom, however you want to look at it." Pain took over the smile in his eyes. Grief flashed and she wondered at it. But instead of explaining his sorrow, he said, "The way I figure it, if God wants you here, who am I to turn you away?"

"God?" She sighed. "What's He got to do with anything?"

Cal's brows tightened over the bridge of his nose. "You don't believe in God?"

"Oh, I believe in Him. I just don't know that I trust Him anymore." She couldn't keep the bitter words from spewing out. But she regretted them the moment they hit his ears. "I'm sorry. I guess God and I have some unresolved issues."

"Sounds like it."

In his eyes, she saw compassion, a warmth that floored her. No judgment, just concern. Who was this man? What made him tick? Why did she thrill at his nearness even as she threw up the barriers to keep him at arm's length?

Mainly because he was a cop, yes. But also because she felt almost guilty being attracted to him, which made no sense.

But it didn't matter.

The bottom line was that she couldn't confide in him. Cops protected each other—even when one of their own was in the wrong. At least that had been her experience. Realistically, she knew that not all cops were like the ones she'd had to deal with, but how could you tell the difference?

And she didn't like learning things the hard way. With a sigh, she rose and walked to the window to stare out at the snow. "How many inches are you supposed to get?"

"Just a couple today. More later." He let her distract him from the intense conversation, but his eyes said they'd revisit it at a later time. "But it's supposed to freeze tonight. So until it warms up later in the afternoon, we'll be kind of stuck in the morning."

She whirled. "What about Fiona? What if the baby decides to come early?" Panic clawed at her throat in spite of Fiona's earlier reassurances.

"Hey." His hands came up to rest on her shoulders. "It's okay. We'll get her to the hospital one way or another. She'll be fine." He shrugged. "Or if she has to have the baby here, Mom's all prepared for that happening."

"But you just said we'd be stuck. Exactly how would she get to the hospital?" She ignored the comment about Fiona having the baby here. That just couldn't be an option.

"Stuck as in not taking any unnecessary chances. If Fiona needs to get to the hospital, we'll get her there. As to the how–" he shrugged "—we'll figure something out."

Abby swallowed hard. No, no, no. That wasn't good enough. She needed him to have a plan, to be ready to put it into action if the baby came early.

But he was saying, "Besides, Mom was a nurse. She can deliver the baby if push comes to shove." He paused, then grinned as his words registered. "Pun intended."

Abby groaned. Not at the pun, but at the thought of Fiona having a home birth.

"Seriously, Fiona will be fine."

His calm confidence caused the overwhelming dread to subside. "Okay, if you say so."

"Why the panic?"

She swallowed, the weight of his hands burning into her shoulders. And feeling right. Good. "That obvious, huh?"

He nodded.

Abby shuddered. "My sister died in childbirth, a home birth," she whispered. "She refused to go to a hospital. When she was seventeen, she was in a horrible car wreck and spent months in the hospital. She's had a crazy fear of them ever since. And she…died. In childbirth. While all I could do was stand there and watch."

A low sound came from him and then his arms were around her pulling her close into his strong embrace. She inhaled the scent that she'd decided belonged exclusively to him and let him offer her comfort. Tried to soak in the peace that exuded from him.

For a moment neither of them moved. Then Abby felt the guilt stab her for taking comfort from Cal when her sister was dead.

Who was holding Reese? Who was offering him solace?

She pulled away and from the corner of her eye caught sight of a flash. She blinked and looked out the window again.

Another flash. Her stomach twisted. "Did you see that?"

Cal looked. "What?"

"There was a flash of something, like the sun reflecting off a metal object. I've noticed it a couple of times today."

He followed her gaze and frowned. "I didn't see anything. You sure?"

She shrugged. "It's probably nothing."

Then they both saw it and Cal jerked her away from the window. Then reached over and closed the blinds.

"What is it?" she asked, alarm spreading through her at his obvious concern.

"I may be overreacting, but I think after your attack, you need to stay away from windows."

"Why?"

"Because until I discover differently, I want you to assume the man who came after you will be back."

Abby gulped as Cal pulled his cell phone from his pocket and pressed a speed dial number. From off to the side, phone pressed to his ear, he used a finger to lift one of the blinds. His eyes intense, he stared out the window. "Zane, check the north pasture up by the ridge where the trees are. See if you find anything—and be careful. I think someone was up there watching the house—either with binoculars or a high-powered rifle scope."

The next morning, when he wanted to be sitting in church worshipping, Cal stared down at the pile of fresh snow covering the tracks that led from trees shading the area in the north pasture. He could see no evidence of it now, but Zane had reported that by the time he got here yesterday, horse tracks had led from the area.

Cal's stomach tightened as he looked toward Fiona's house. Squatting, he had a perfect view of the kitchen window. With the blinds open and a pair of binoculars, he'd have no trouble seeing straight inside.

Foreboding filled him. He had a feeling whoever had been up here watching had more on his mind than spying.

Just like before, he was scoping, watching, learning the routine.

Cal rubbed his jaw as he considered how to best defend his family, his land—and Abby.

He'd had his fair share of trouble in the past. He'd arrested would-be horse thieves once. Run off a few harmless vagrants looking for a place to set up camp for a while. But for the most part, his ranch was a peaceful place.

And he intended to keep it that way.

After Abby's incident yesterday, Cal had called in to request some time off. Fortunately, the sheriff's department was fully staffed right now and taking this personal time wouldn't be a hardship on the other deputies who would cover his shift.

Eli Brody, sheriff of Rose Mountain and a good friend to Cal and his family, promised to keep an eye out for someone who didn't fit in. Although he'd given a snort of disgust and said, "Of course you know how it is this time of year. So many strangers in town I might not spot the guy you're after."

"I know. He might not even be in town. He could be camping out somewhere on my property and I'd never know it unless I stumbled over him by accident. Three-thousand acres is a lot of ground to cover, but I've got the guys out there, watching. It's all we can do right now."

"Well, just be careful. Let me know if you need any backup."

"Will do."

Armed with the knowledge that Eli was keeping his eyes open in town, Cal hung up only to have his phone buzz once more.

Zane.

"What is it?"

"The horses are out of the fence." His foreman's tight

voice cut into Cal's musing over who had been on his property.

"How?" he asked even as he swung back into Snickers's saddle.

"I was on my way up to check on that mare that's ready to foal and found the fence cut—again—and the horses scattering."

A cold feeling settled in the pit of his stomach. Some of those horses didn't belong to him. He boarded some of those animals for the extra income. If any of them got hurt or lost... He shuddered to think of the cost. Not just to his pocket, but to his reputation. The ranch would go under.

"Gather Donny, Mike and Jesse and start rounding them up. I'm on my way."

Abby looked up from the computer to see Fiona looking through the cabinet for something. The woman had wanted to go to church this morning, but had been voted down by her mother and Cal. They were too worried about her making an unnecessary trip through the snow and ice. She'd argued that the ice would be melted by the time the late service started, but had finally agreed to stay put.

Frankly, Abby silently agreed with them and been relieved when Fiona caved. "Why don't you move closer to the hospital until the baby comes?" Abby couldn't help asking.

Fiona turned to look at her. "Because this is my home. People have babies all the time. If I were a high risk, I'd do it, but I'm not. My blood pressure's fine, the baby is fine." She shrugged. "There's no reason."

"But it's just a precaution," Abby argued.

"I know—"

Fiona broke off when the phone rang.

Abby turned back to the computer until Fiona gasped. Spinning around, Abby took in the tight, frantic look on the woman's face. Abby's heart skipped a beat and she asked, "What's wrong? Are you okay? Is it the baby?"

Fiona grabbed her coat from the rack. "No, the horses are loose. We've got to get them back in the fence or they could end up who knows where."

Alarmed, Abby bolted to her feet. She'd been working on the files again at the kitchen table using the laptop Cal had given her last night. "You can't go out there. I'll help."

Fiona gripped the coat in her fist. "I have to."

"No. Think of the baby."

That stopped her. She pulled in a deep breath even as she bowed her head in defeat. "I know I can't," she whispered, "but the horses…we can't lose any of them. They're not all ours. Our clients depend on us to keep their animals safe."

Abby didn't hesitate. She hurried down the steps to her small apartment and snatched the heavy down coat, hat and gloves from the chair. Bless Fiona's heart in loaning them to her. She raced back up the stairs to find Fiona still in the kitchen, looking out the window, her face reflecting her anxiety. Abby told her, "I can round up horses as well as the next person. I've done it before."

Surprise took the place of some of Fiona's worry. "Really?"

"Yep."

Then the frown returned. "But you're still recovering."

Abby tugged on the coat, then the gloves. "I'm fine.

Not a hundred percent, maybe, but definitely okay to go hunt some horses."

Gratitude flared in Fiona's eyes. "I'll call the barn and have Jesse saddle you a mount—if Jesse's still there."

"If not, I can do it myself."

Abby opened the door and stepped out into the cold. The temperatures hovered in the low forties, melting the ice that had formed the night before. Still, a strong wind blew and she shivered as she trudged toward the barn.

At least it had stopped snowing, although the sky threatened more.

Entering the barn, she paused, taking in the smell of hay and horses. She saw Jesse slipping the bridal on a beautiful quarter horse.

Another fully tacked horse had been tied to the post about ten feet away. Jesse looked at her. "Here ya go. Ms. Fiona caught me just as I was heading out. This little darlin' is Pretty Mama. She's got a good temperament. You won't have any problems outta her." Several harnesses were hooked to the saddle. She knew she'd use those to lead whatever horses she was able to snag back to the pasture.

"Thanks, Jesse." Abby took the reins from him and introduced herself to the horse by slipping her a couple of sugar cubes she'd snitched from the kitchen.

Jessed watched her with a twinkle in his eye. "Know yer way around horses, eh?"

"A bit." Abby smiled and hauled herself into the saddle. It felt good. And right. She shifted and got comfortable on the creaking leather, thankful she no longer had a headache or dizziness. "Where should we look first?"

"I'd say around the river, but honestly, they could be anywhere by now. Cal said he was heading back this way to check the creek line." He shook his head. "That river's high right now with all the rain and snow we've had. Temperatures are melting the ice, but the river's edge will still be frozen and slick. Be careful around it."

"I will." She adjusted the stirrups as she mentally pictured the direction she'd go from the barn.

Jesse said, "I'm hoping those horses will stick together. Fortunately, it's not like they're wild. You should be able to ride right up to 'em and slip a harness over their heads."

Clicking to the horse, Abby guided her from the barn. Together, she and Jesse headed toward the river. Unfamiliar with the land, she visualized the layout of the ranch in her mind using the map she'd seen on the wall in the den.

They rode slow and easy for the next few minutes.

"I see one," Jesse said. "I'm heading that way." He pointed to the black horse in the distance. Abby nodded and watched him gallop away.

She turned back toward the river and felt a shiver ride up her spine. Feeling exposed, she hurried toward the tree line telling herself she was being silly and yet unable to squelch the desire to be behind some kind of cover. With the attack still fresh in her mind, she suddenly didn't want to be alone.

Then she spotted movement down near the river through a grove of trees. If the trees had had leaves on them, she never would have seen it. Then the brown and white horse walked to the edge of the river, then a little farther to get past the ice. He stuck his nose in the water to have a drink.

Nudging the horse with her heels, she said, "Come

on, Pretty Mama, let's go see if we can get a lead on your friend there."

Pretty Mama responded and they headed down the small hill. In the distance she could see a man leading three other horses in her direction. Zane? It looked like him.

At the edge of the trees, Abby stopped, the hair on the back of her neck standing up. A spot between her shoulders itched.

She glanced around.

Nothing there to give her any reason to feel like she had a target on her back. On this side of the ranch, about a mile from Fiona's house, she knew she wasn't far from the main road that led into the town of Rose Mountain.

Another horse came into sight, stretching its silky brown neck to lap at the water. The river was lazy, not a rushing fast-paced body of water and Abby knew for Cal and his family, it was a priceless commodity to have.

And while it all looked peaceful, she couldn't shake the feeling of being watched.

"Just get the horses and get back," she muttered to herself.

Looking back over her shoulder, she saw the man leading the other three horses disappear out of sight as he rode down the hill that led to the barn.

She shivered, not just from the chill of the forty-degree weather, but from the sheer isolation she now found herself in.

Ignoring her troubled thoughts, she focused on the horses. It was a small thing to do for the family who'd taken her in and nursed her back to health.

"Come on, Pretty Mama, let's go."

Abby walked the horse closer, pulling one of the halters from the hook on her saddle. The paint raised its head and snorted at her but didn't try to run. Abby slid from the saddle and snitched an apple from her saddle bag. She looped Pretty Mama's reins over the nearest tree and approached the other horse. She'd focus on this one, then go for the one farther down.

"Hey, pretty boy, you want an apple?" She hoped the croon in her voice would keep the horse calm, settled. He didn't know her and she wasn't sure how he felt about strangers.

He stomped a foot and leaned down for another drink, walking part of the way into the river to get even farther past the frozen edges.

The water had to be freezing, but the horse didn't seem to mind. She noted the shallow area where the animal stood and wondered if the river was deeper farther out, closer to the middle, or if it was the same depth all the way across.

Must be deeper because it wasn't frozen solid.

The back of her neck tingled and she jerked her gaze from the horse to look behind her. Nothing but trees.

So where was her uneasiness coming from?

Leftover from yesterday's attack probably.

Get the horse. Focus. You can do this simple thing. A small thing as part of a way to say thanks to the Mc-Ivers for all they've done for you.

Abby edged closer to the horse, one foot carefully placed in front of the other as she made her way down to the river.

A blast of wind skimmed off the surface of the water and hit her full in the face. She gasped and shivered but didn't let it stop her. Keeping her eyes on the horse, she whispered sweet nothings to him. He eyed her and swished his tail, but other than that, didn't seem bothered by her presence.

Unfortunately, he'd moved into the water and to get ahold of his head to slip the halter and lead on, she'd have to step into the river.

She paused, debating. Her boots were water-resistant but were short. The river would flow right over the top of them.

"Come here, boy. Come here." Staying well out of kicking range, she patted the horse's rump. He sidestepped her, but at least he backed up a bit.

She grasped the bottom part of his mane and pulled his head around.

Then something slammed into her back and she felt herself lifted, pulled backward.

Letting out a startled scream, Abby tried to turn to face whatever had ahold of her. The startled horse bucked and bolted at the sudden action.

Abby jerked back, twisted and pulled away.

She must have surprised her attacker with her desperate moves because he let go and she was free. Turning, she came face to face with a man in a ski mask.

Wordless, he reached for her again, his fingers wrapping around her wrist.

"Let me go!" she screamed at him. "Leave me alone, Reese!

The fingers loosened and Abby felt her feet fly out from under her. Off balance, she stumbled, desperately tried to right herself and overcompensated. She went down hard.

Right into the icy water.

SIX

Cal heard the commotion, then the splash as he came over the rise. Then thundering hoofbeats as two of his horses tore across the open field, heading for the edge of the property.

Frowning, Cal saw the horse Abby had been riding tied to the tree, another horse partway in the water about ten yards away from her.

And Abby doing her best to get to the bank.

"Oh, no." She'd be a candidate for serious hypothermia if he didn't get her out of there fast. "Abby!" The river was deeper than it looked in some places.

Looked like she'd found that out the hard way.

The dangerous way.

Déjà vu flittered across his mind as he raced toward her. Fear for her choked him even as he thought he might have to keep her under lock and key to make sure she stayed out of danger.

He rode his horse straight into the shallow part of the river, his mount's hooves crunching through the frozen ice. Cal pulled the stallion to a halt at the edge. Any farther and the horse might not be able to get out. "Abby!"

She struggled to get her feet under her, the water was

only about four-feet deep, but the temperature was probably around fifteen degrees.

He'd jump in and grab her if he didn't know he'd find himself in as much trouble with the cold water as she was. He'd need to keep himself strong to help her.

Abby spotted him and her eyes showed mammoth proportions of relief even while her movements grew sluggish. "Cal!"

Willing his heart to settle, he pulled a rope from the side of his saddle and tossed it to her. "Slip that under your arms."

Her gloved hands flopped, tried to grasp it and couldn't get it. "Can't." Panic flared. "It's…too hard… to move."

"Abby, listen to me! You have to. Grab it!" he ordered, his voice harsh, demanding. "Now!"

She flinched and made another effort, this time getting her wrist through the loop and sluggishly shoving it up to her shoulder.

Cal pulled the rope tight, praying it was enough to keep her attached until he could get her out of the water. He was running out of time.

Clicking to Snickers, he backed the horse up with his knees and one hand on the reins. The other hand pulled the rope, taking up the slack and dragging her toward the edge of the river.

So far so good. "Hang on, Abby."

Almost there.

Finally, he dropped the rope and bolted from the saddle into the shallower knee-deep water. He gasped and shuddered at the frigid bite but ignored it as he got his hands under her arms.

Cal pulled her onto the bank. Snickers whickered and tossed his head.

Cal grabbed his cell phone from the pocket of his bag attached to the saddle and called Zane. "I need someone on standby for emergency hypothermia treatment." He hung up, not bothering to explain. "Abby, look at me."

Her teeth chattered. A good sign. Her body was still able to react to the cold. If she stopped shivering, he'd be more worried.

"S-s-so cold."

"I know. We're going to get you warmed up." His mind raced as he filtered through all he knew about hypothermia. Getting her dry and warm were the priorities.

The rumble of a truck caught his attention, then the wheels crunching through snow and some still-frozen ice. Zane.

The man pulled up beside the trees and he burst from the cab. "What happened?"

"Not sure. Let's get her back to the house and warmed up before we start pumping her for information."

Zane nodded. Cal picked Abby up, and grunted. The heavy clothes soaked with the cold water added quite a few pounds to her normally slight frame.

Together, he and Zane maneuvered her into the backseat of the King cab. Cal climbed in with her and helped her get out of her soggy coat and boots.

His mother could help with the rest when he got her to the house. Pulling out his cell phone, he dialed his mother's number. By the time she answered on the third ring, Cal's patience was just about used up.

He told her what he needed and hung up. Within seconds, Zane pulled up beside the small apartment and parked.

Fiona and his mother met them at the door. Little

Tiffany hovered beside his mother. When she saw her grandfather, she reached for him.

"Hold on, baby," Zane said. "We've got to get Miss Abby warmed up."

The little girl stepped back, curious eyes wide, taking in every detail of the action before her.

Working quickly, Cal got Abby inside. She reached up and grabbed his hand in her ice cold one. "Someone pushed me," she whispered.

Cal felt his heart stop, then speed up like a freight train out of control. "Who? Why?"

"I d-d-don't know."

And then Cal's mother and Fiona shooed the men out. Cal gave Abby one last lingering look as he stepped back.

Her pale white face and blue-tinged lips struck something in him he'd never felt before.

He shut the door and stood still, head bowed.

With his sister, his mother…Brianne, he felt protective, wanting to take care of them, make sure they had everything they needed and that they were safe from harm.

Of course Fiona now had Joseph to fill that role.

With Abby, those protective feelings were also there, but it was more than just feeling protective. A murderous rage against the person who dared to invade his home, his property, those under his protection stirred in his gut.

Cal clenched a gloved fist as he headed toward his home to change his boots and pants.

He'd catch this person and then make sure he was punished to the fullest extent of the law—and if the law wouldn't do anything about it, he had friends who would.

* * *

Abby couldn't remember being this cold since...ever. She'd never been this cold. The physician part of her brain took over as she took a mental inventory.

Now in dry clothes and propped up in the recliner with her feet on the ottoman, she had her hands wrapped around a hot cup of coffee.

Slowly the warmth of the mug penetrated the ice that had become her hands.

Her muscles were less sluggish, her mind a little more clear. She would be all right.

As soon as she thawed out.

Fiona and her sweet mother hovered. She looked at them and said, "Thank you for coming to my rescue once again."

"Our pleasure, dear." The words were sincere, but Abby couldn't help notice the worried frown pulling the woman's brows together at the bridge of her nose.

Abby took another sip of the steaming yet now-drinkable coffee. "I don't know what I would have done if Cal hadn't come along when he did."

"Who pushed you?"

Fiona's gentle question made Abby blink. Right. She'd blurted that out to Cal. Her next shiver had nothing to do with the chill she still felt to her bones. "I don't know. He had on a ski mask."

"Why is this person coming after you?" Cal's mother asked. "You're welcome to stay here as long as you need, but if there's danger...well, the McIvers have never run from it, but we'd like to be prepared for it."

Fiona nodded.

And Abby felt about two inches tall.

She opened her mouth to spill her story when a knock sounded on the door. Fiona opened it to let Cal in.

Abby bit her lip. She'd almost forgotten. Cal was a cop. Cops stuck together. If she spilled her guts, he'd never believe her brother-in-law was behind the attacks on her life.

In fact, if Reese hadn't uttered those horrible, threatening words while standing at his wife's deathbed, she wouldn't believe it herself.

But he had.

"How are you doing?" Cal asked as he pulled the door shut behind him.

She nodded. "Warming up. You?"

"I put on two pairs of socks. I think my toes are about thawed." He flashed her a grin, and she couldn't stop the answering smile or the rapid flutter of her heart as she wondered what he'd do if she grabbed him and pulled him down for a thank-you kiss. Heat immediately infused her face.

Well, that was one way to get warm, she thought ruefully. Just think about kissing Callum McIvers.

Instead, she derailed that thought when his smile flipped into a frown. "Did you know that man at the river?"

Shaking her head, she glanced at the McIver family. "No. I was just telling your mother and Fiona that he had a ski mask on. I couldn't tell a thing about him." She paused. "Other than the fact that he was strong. But lean. Not really muscular and not really that much taller than I am." Which was really odd, she mused slowly, because Reese Kirkpatrick was a tall man topping six feet easily. Maybe even an inch or two over.

So what did that mean?

The man who attacked her wasn't Reese?

Then who had Reese paid to attack her?

"And you said he pushed you."

She gathered the rest of her thoughts. "Yes." Frowned again. "No."

Cal grunted. "Well, which is it?"

Abby shook her head. "I'm sorry. It's just that…I thought I felt someone watching me, but couldn't see anyone. There were several horses in that area. I was focused on the paint drinking from the river."

Cal nodded his encouragement. "And?"

"Well, the horse was in the river. In the shallow part. I got off my horse thinking it might be easier to get a lead on the paint if I wasn't leaning over my own horse. Only the paint was kind of stubborn and didn't want to come out of the water."

"That's Shoes for you. Stubborn as they come."

"Anyway, I got up to him and almost had the halter with the lead on him when I felt something grab the back of my coat and pull me around." Abby swallowed at the memory. The nightmare of coming face to face with the masked man. "He didn't say anything, just pulled me. I yanked away from him, he lost his grip and I went into the river." She finished the last part of the sentence slowly. "Actually, I guess he didn't really push me. I…fell."

"But if he hadn't been there, you wouldn't have fallen."

"True." Another shiver racked her frame.

A loud crash came from upstairs and Cal darted to his feet, hand on his gun.

With a quick look at the women, he said, "Stay here."

SEVEN

Cal took the steps two at a time. No one was supposed to be here. At the top of the steps, he paused, pushed the door open a crack. Just enough to peer around and into the kitchen.

Muttering reached his ears.

His fingers gripped his weapon…

…then he relaxed.

"What are you doing home?" he asked.

Joseph looked up, his blue eyes startled. "Cal? I finished up a day early and caught a flight this morning. What are you doing in my basement? And where's Fiona? Is she all right?"

Cal laughed and before his brother-in-law could see the move, he turned slightly and slid his gun back into the holster. "Fiona's fine. What's all the racket up here?"

Joseph shook his head. "I stopped and got some groceries. Figured with this storm coming, we might need 'em. When I put them on the counter, I knocked over the cookie jar."

Only then did Cal notice the sacks of food—and the spilled cookies Joseph was cleaning up. Cal snagged one and popped it in his mouth. "Did Fiona tell you about our visitor?"

"Yeah, she texted me." He smirked. "Passed out right in your arms, so I hear."

Ignoring the teasing and the flush he could feel creeping up the back of his neck, Cal nodded and walked to the top of the stairs. "Hey, Fiona, Joseph's here."

"Joseph?" His sister's excited voice responded. Then he heard her footsteps. She appeared at the bottom of the steps, then began climbing, her right hand grasping the rail.

Joseph brushed past him and met her halfway to walk back up the steps, his hand on her back. Cal smiled. Now that she was pregnant, Joseph treated his wife like she was as fragile as fine porcelain. He could tell it grated on Fiona's nerves occasionally, but Fiona knew he meant well.

"We had a little incident this morning. Abby fell in the river," Fiona said.

"What?" Joseph frowned. "How did that happen?"

Cal explained. At the end of the story, Joseph shook his head, his mouth tight. "Domestic violence? She name the guy yet?"

Cal shook his head. "No. She's too scared and she hasn't known us long enough to trust us with that kind of thing yet."

"Maybe if you tell her about Brianne, she'd be more inclined to open up," Cal's mother said from the top of the stairs.

She walked into the kitchen and everyone fell silent. Fiona looked at Cal. "You're the one she really needs to trust because you're the one who can do something about it. If she tells mom or me something in confidence…"

"You'd be obliged to keep it. I understand that." Cal blew out a breath and vowed to do his best to get Abby to trust him.

* * *

Three days passed without any more frightening incidents. Abby continued to regain her strength. Each day the weather warmed to just above freezing and the snow started to melt, only to freeze again in the overnight lows. Cal left to head into town to work a shift for a deputy who'd called in sick.

Abby knew he felt better about leaving now that Joseph was there to keep watch and he couldn't take time off infinitely. Fiona's husband was officially off work until after the arrival of his son and the passing of the holidays.

And each day, Abby came to love this little family more. Her heart especially seemed to be attached to Cal. He invaded her dreams when she slept and her thoughts when she was awake.

And Abby decided she'd better leave the McIvers while she could.

But how?

Did the small town of Rose Mountain have a taxi service?

Probably not.

She looked at the screen on the borrowed laptop and an idea formed while thoughts of leaving were put on hold. She'd been diligent about searching the medical records she'd copied onto the flash drive.

And she'd found some conflicting information. However, she needed to access her work computer. The only problem was if someone knew she was doing it, she'd be easy to trace because she'd have to go through her account. Which would mean leaving a traceable footprint behind.

Although she thought she might not need to worry

about that as it looked like Reese knew where she was. So, really, why bother to worry about it?

However, the fact that he'd been quiet the past few days made her nervous. Like she was waiting for the proverbial other shoe to drop.

Or another attack to occur.

And what if this time he didn't confine it to just her? What if he decided he didn't care who he hurt and the McIvers family got caught in the cross fire?

Biting her lip, she clicked her way into the program that would give her remote access to her work computer.

As soon as she logged into her work program, she could be tracked.

Taking a deep breath, she decided the risk was worth it. Especially if she found the information she needed. She would grab it and run. Lead Reese away from the McIvers family and they would be safe.

Decision made, she continued to click, put in her user name and password and within a second had access to her work computer.

Navigating around the software was second nature and before long she was knee-deep in reading, comparing the information to what she'd copied on the flash drive. She frowned, unsure if she was seeing what she thought she was.

"What are you doing?"

Abby jumped and spun to see Fiona standing in the doorway to the kitchen. Abby had come upstairs to work and have access to the printer. She smiled at the woman who placed a hand on her lower back and grimaced.

"Hey, are you all right?"

Fiona nodded. "Junior here is really active today. I

tried to take a nap and he punched and kicked me until I got up to move around. Now he's decided to go to sleep."

Abby studied her. "You've dropped."

"Huh?"

Abby laughed. "The baby. He's moved lower, you're not carrying him as high."

"That's good, right?"

"Definitely. It means he's getting ready to announce his presence to the world. Can you breathe better?"

Fiona laughed and cocked her head. "You know, I can. And just this morning I ate breakfast and didn't get heartburn for the first time in months."

Abby nodded knowingly. But then her gut twisted as she remembered the forecast. Snow, snow and more snow. And freezing temperatures.

Even though it wouldn't be a problem right now, the closer Fiona got to her delivery date, the more Abby worried.

She had to leave.

A door slammed and Fiona waddled out of the kitchen to the front of the house. "Joseph?"

Footsteps stomped toward her and then Joseph stood in the kitchen, his face tight, anger lighting his blue eyes as he looked at Abby.

Unease gripped her. "What is it? Why are you looking at me like that?"

He held up his right hand and she saw his fingers wrapped around a piece of paper. "This just came. Addressed to me and my wife."

Abby stood and took a step forward. "Okay. And why does it have you looking at me like you'd like to rip my head from my shoulders?"

She knew that look. Reese had glared at her with that very same expression the day his wife died. When the coroner had pried his baby girl from his arms after one last anguished goodbye.

"Joseph, what in the world?" Fiona looked shocked at her husband's actions.

"Because," Joseph bit out, ignoring his wife, "it says that you're a—" He shoved the letter at her. "Read it yourself, then get out of my house."

"Joseph Whitley!" Fiona's outraged cry caught his attention.

His face never softened. "You'll understand in a minute."

Abby's heartbeat tripled, her hands shook and she didn't even know what she was going to read. She just knew it was about her and that it was bad.

As her eyes flowed over the words, the trembling started from deep within.

Aloud, she read, "Dear Whitley family, I'm sure you meant well by taking in the woman, Abigail O'Sullivan. However, I feel it's my duty to warn you just who you've allowed into your home. Abby is a murderer, a cold-blooded killer. A baby killer who hasn't been brought to justice. You'd do well to get rid of her before you regret it. Sincerely, Reese Kirkpatrick."

Abby felt numb, sick, angry and hopeless all at the same time. The paper slid from her fingers and hit the floor.

"Would someone please tell me what's going on? And her name's not O'Sullivan, it's Harris." Fiona's trouble expression sent shards of pain shooting through Abby's heart.

She bent down and picked up the paper. Without a word she handed it to the woman she'd come to care for as a friend. "I…lied about my name. I'm so sorry. I have no excuse except that I was…afraid. I'll go get my things." To Joseph, she said, "Would you mind giving me a ride to the bus station?"

His cold eyes pierced her. "My pleasure."

Cal's internal alarm kept nagging him. He rubbed the back of his neck and sighed. From his own desk across the room, Eli looked at him. "Problem?"

"I don't know. Maybe."

"Wanna talk about it?"

Cal shrugged. "It's Abby. I'm not sure what her story is and I think I really need to know." He sighed and pinched the bridge of his nose.

"You can always do a background check on her."

Troubled, Cal nodded. "I know. I've considered it. The thing is, I don't think she's done anything wrong. I think she's on the run from someone and I don't know how to gain her trust. She seems to be pretty comfortable with me until I ask her a personal question."

He told Eli about calling Abby's mother and the cold reception and rejection of Abby. "By her own mother," he said. "Hard to imagine someone could just turn their back on their own kid like that." But in his profession, he'd seen his share of rotten parents. Still, it bothered him.

Eli shook his head. "I know. I can't think of anything my son would do that would make me disown him." He grinned. "Of course he's almost two, so we'll see."

"The terrible twos?"

"Holly always has an interesting story for me when I get home. That boy is stubborn. He wanted to try and swim in the toilet. Pitched a fit when she wouldn't let him."

Cal choked on a laugh, then grunted. "Comes by it naturally with you two for parents."

"You just wait." Eli narrowed his eyes. "You'll find out one day."

That pronouncement immediately brought to mind Abby in a white dress, a church and a couple of rings.

And an infant in her arms.

His heart thundered in his chest and he swallowed hard. Watch out, buddy, you don't even know this woman's background and you're already walking down the aisle and imagining children.

His cell phone buzzed. Fiona.

"Hello?"

"Cal! You've got to do something, quick!"

All senses on alert, he sat straight up. "What is it? What's wrong?"

"It's Abby!" He listened as she spilled some awful nonsense about Abby being a baby killer and Joseph being angry.

"And she's on her way to the bus station?"

Eli listened, gaze sharp, showing a readiness to jump into action should it be needed.

"I'll take care of it." Cal hung up and bolted to his feet. He looked at Eli. "Do that background check, will you?"

Abby stepped out of Joseph's truck. She looked at him.

"It's not what it sounds like."

Joseph's eyes softened for a moment. "That may be true. But I can't take that chance. I have to protect my family."

"Protect your family from what?"

Cal's growl whipped her head around. The thunderous look on his face didn't look good.

Abby grabbed her bag from the floor of the cab. "From me."

Tossing the bag over her shoulder, she tromped toward the bus station.

"Abby, wait!" she heard him holler. She wanted nothing more than to turn around and run into his arms. Then she heard him demand, "Joseph, what's this all about?"

The hair on the back of her neck rose, and she couldn't help giving the area around her a glance. Nothing seemed out of place or suspicious, but she couldn't help wondering if her attacker was somewhere nearby, watching, waiting for her to be all alone.

Well, he wouldn't have to wait long.

A blast of frigid wind compelled her to hurry inside the station. Absently, she noted the snowflakes that had started to fall once again. Big heavy flakes.

A hand on her arm spun her around just inside the door. "You don't have to leave," Cal told her.

"Yes, I do." She pulled away from him and walked toward a bench.

"I saw the letter." He paused. "I don't believe a word of it, but I'd like an explanation as to why someone dislikes you so much he'd write it. Don't you think you owe me that much?"

Probably. Actually she owed him much more, but she just couldn't bring herself to trust him no matter how much she wanted to. Vision of Reese's buddies watching her, waiting for her wherever she went flitted through her mind. Pulling her over and giving her a warning for some made-up infraction of the law.

Cops stuck together. No matter what. At least the ones she knew did.

Maybe Cal was different. But could she take that chance? "I do owe you, I just…I'm afraid…"

His hand reached out to stroke her hair. She wanted to lean into the comfort. He cupped her chin. "Who do you need protection from?"

She looked away. "It doesn't matter. Just leave me alone and let me go." She set her jaw and headed to the counter.

"Abby, please…" His soft voice stopped her in her tracks.

Closing her eyes, she drew in a deep breath. Looking around, she spotted an empty bench and motioned him toward it. They sat side by side, her bag resting against her legs. "That horrible letter is a lie. And yet…it's not."

Confusion clouded his eyes. "You're no murderer, Abby."

She felt tears press against her eyelids. It was too soon to tell him. Too raw to talk about. "Like I told you, my sister died in childbirth. And so did her baby. My family blames me for not being able to convince her to go to the hospital."

He blew a raspberry. "How is that your fault? She was a grown woman capable of making her own decisions, was she not?"

A little humorless laugh escaped her. "Yes, of course. It's just that my family and her husband thought that I should have been able to 'talk some sense into her.'" She wiggled her fingers as imaginary quotes as she said the last five words.

Only she wasn't telling him the whole story. Wasn't adding that she'd been her sister's doctor. Was supposed to deliver a healthy baby girl so she and Keira and Reese could live happily ever after.

Cal didn't look like he was buying her story.

But it was the truth.

Most of it anyway.

"You're leaving something out."

Biting her lip, she nodded. "Some things hurt too much to talk about," she whispered.

"Yeah, I know." He sighed and his eyes took on a far-away look. And she realized that he might understand if she told him the rest of it.

Then the light winked off his badge and the words froze in her throat.

She couldn't confide in him. Not yet. Maybe not ever.

"I'm sorry."

"Come on back to the house," he said with a glance to the glass door. "It's snowing buckets now. Whatever bus you're wanting to take is going to be stuck anyway."

She gasped and looked.

Once again, a world of white greeted her. Abby jumped up from the bench and grabbed her bag. "I've got to get my ticket."

"Where are you going?"

She wrinkled her nose. "Somewhere warm." She walked toward the ticket counter and got in line.

Cal followed. "Abby, come home with me. Please."

"I can't." She kept her voice low. "Joseph doesn't trust me. Not around Fiona. Not after that letter." She swallowed hard. "And I don't blame him."

"I trust you."

She stared at him. "How can you say that? You don't know me. You don't know—" Could she even say it? "I was— I let her die, Cal. I watched her stop breathing, I tried everything I knew how to do and it wasn't good enough. I let her die!" Tears welled, threatened to rupture into a flood she'd never be able to stem.

He pulled her into his arms. They felt so good so she

didn't have the strength to fight him. "Abby, honey, I'm so sorry."

She looked up at him, the grief nearly crippling her. "So? You see?" She whispered. "You don't know. I should have stopped it. I should have known what to do. But I…"

Even as his fingers swiped the tears from under her eyes, he was saying, "I know enough. And I have great instincts when it comes to reading people. Yeah, I think you're keeping secrets, but you're no killer and you're not a danger to my family—no matter what Joseph thinks." He gestured to the door. "Do you really want to be out in that? On your own? With someone after you?"

Abby gulped. "Not really."

"Stay with us, Abby. Let me help you."

She studied him in wonder. "Why do you care?" she whispered.

Cal smiled a slow, gentle pull of his lips. "Because it's been a really long time since I've met a woman who makes me feel…what you make me feel…when you walk into the room—or give me a genuine smile." He shrugged and she saw his cheeks take on a reddish tinge. "I'm not ready to see you leave yet. I want to get to know you better."

Abby gulped. Did he really just say that? Should she tell him the feeling was mutual? With a sinking feeling, she decided that once he knew her better, he wouldn't want anything to do with her. Not after he learned who her brother-in-law was. Not after Reese got through telling Cal how she'd failed them all. Not after he learned she was her sister's doctor.

And what about the person following her? Looking around she still didn't see anyone even though the feeling of being watched never left her. Could she risk Cal's family?

"I can't, Cal. So far, this person has come after only me. What if he decides to change that? What if he doesn't care who he hurts?" She gulped. "If something happened to you or Fiona or…I couldn't live with myself."

And if her attacker was Reese—or someone he hired—he would know a lot of ways to hurt people.

"Let me worry about that. I'm a cop. I can handle this, believe it or not. And I don't have to do it alone. I have friends and experienced backup to help."

Abby studied him, noting his rugged, good-looking features, his strong jaw and determined eyes. She had no doubt that he would do his best to protect her. And that scared her. Even strong, capable men got killed. And she didn't know exactly who was after her. If it was Reese, hardheaded, stubborn, unforgiving Reese… "I don't mean to imply that you can't. It's just…"

His eyes never wavered from hers. He wasn't going to force her, but he wasn't going to take no for an answer.

She sighed. Looked outside one more time—and caved. "All right."

He pulled her into a hug. "Now I'm going to get the car and have a heart-to-heart with Joseph. You stay by the door and wait for me to pull up." Already there was at least an inch of snow on the ground and the temperature was dropping. She looked at the board. And buses were being canceled.

Going home with Cal suddenly seemed like the best thing to do right now.

She'd just have to stay out of Joseph's way.

EIGHT

Cal couldn't help the huge burst of relief that ruptured through him when he was finally able to talk Abby into going back to the ranch with him. He couldn't explain it, either, except that he'd been honest with her. She made him feel things he hadn't felt in a long time.

Those feelings unnerved him but excited him all at the same time. He had to admit watching Joseph and Fiona and his friends, Eli and Holly, and Dylan and Paige succumb to love, marriage and family had him yearning for the same.

Joseph waited in his truck, his jaw tight, eyes on Cal. Cal blinked as the snow hit him in the face and tugged the collar of his coat tighter.

Joseph rolled down the window as Cal approached. "She leaving?"

"Nope. She's coming home with me."

Anger flashed in his brother-in-law's eyes. "You saw that letter, Cal. How can you justify bringing her back to the house?"

"If you'd rather her not stay with you and Fiona, she can stay with Mom. That letter is a lie. It has to be."

Joseph's fingers tapped the wheel as he thought. Cal waited, wishing the man would hurry up. He was freezing and he wanted to get back to the office. His shift wasn't over for a couple of hours. Abby could hang out in the local café and wait on him. He didn't think it would be a good idea to ask Joseph to take her home.

"Well? You gonna think all day?"

Joseph sighed and lost his mutinous expression. "You're sure about this?"

Cal nodded. "Yep."

"How sure?"

"A hundred percent. I think I'm falling for her."

The expression on Joseph's face made Cal laugh out loud. He couldn't believe he'd allowed those words to pass his lips, but it was too late to take them back.

Abby saw Joseph drive off and breathed a sigh of relief. She couldn't believe Cal had talked her into going back to the ranch with him. But he had.

Because she really didn't want to leave him. She was drawn to him and his lovely family. She wanted to get to know him, too. Trust him with her secrets, her pain.

But once she did, would he shove her away? If there was any hope for a future together, that was one thing she was going to have to find out.

Cal motioned to her to hop in the front seat of the cruiser. She opened the door and tossed her bag on the floor.

Cal said, "Why don't I drop you at John's Café?" Abby knew the little restaurant sat on one side of John's General Store. On the other side was The Candy Caper, according to Fiona. "Actually, I have a better idea." Pulling his cell phone from his clip, he dialed a number.

"Holly, this is Cal. I have a friend who's waiting for me to get off duty. Do you have time to keep her company?"

What was he doing?

"Great. Great. See you then." Hanging up, he looked at her with a smug grin. "Do you like candy?"

She blinked. "Sure."

"Then you'll love this."

Wondering if the man had lost his mind, Abby didn't protest as he drove her down Main Street and pulled into the parking lot of The Candy Caper. A pretty green wreath with a red bow hung on the door. Lights were strung along the gutter and Abby could picture them lit up at night. A Christmas tree winked and blinked beyond the glass window just inside the store.

A petite young woman with blond hair and blue eyes peered out through the glass door. Seeing them, she smiled. A dart of jealousy fired through Abby and she clamped down on it.

Cal said, "I'd take you with me, but I don't think you'd enjoy it very much. Holly is Eli Brody's wife. Eli's the sheriff here in town. I think you and Holly would get along great."

The jealousy faded and she felt silly. Hoping he didn't notice the red she knew was in her cheeks, she opened the door. Cal stopped her when his hand grabbed hers. "Be careful. Watch your back. I'll try to drive by. Might even be able to come sit with you for a while. But we've got some teenagers who think they're tough and are causing problems at the high school. I need to ride over there and put in an appearance."

"The high school doesn't have a full-time SRO?"

"School Resource Officer? No, unfortunately, we don't. It's a goal, though. If those kids weren't causing trouble, I could stay with you."

She nodded. "It's not a big deal, Cal. Go do your job." Looking around, she shivered, trying not to be paranoid, scared. "I'll be fine." Abby forced a smile she felt quite sure Cal saw right through. But he simply lifted a finger to stroke her cheek leaving a heated trail in its wake.

Abby scrambled out of the car, grabbing her bag from the floor. She looked up to find Holly still watching from the door, her brow raised and a small smile playing around her lips.

Holly opened the store door for her and Abby stepped inside the shop. A variety of scents assailed her. Chocolate, cinnamon, vanilla. Her stomach rumbled.

"Hi, Abby, I'm Holly."

Abby watched Cal wave and drive off. Turning, she smiled at the woman. "Hi. Nice to meet you."

"Would you like some hot chocolate? A cappuccino?"

"Hot chocolate sounds great."

Holly went to work fixing the drinks. "I've just started serving gourmet coffees and offering some healthy choices for lunches. I only have five choices on the lunch menu, so it keeps it pretty simple."

"That sounds lovely. And you run the shop, too? Wow."

"Yes." Holly laughed. "It's a lot of work. I've hired a few extra people to work some different shifts so that I can have time off and don't have to work every minute of every day."

"How long have you lived in Rose Mountain?"

"All my life." Holly handed Abby the mug of hot chocolate and motioned to a small section of the store that had a seating area.

Abby dropped her bag by the chair and made sure she could see the door. The way things had been going lately, she wouldn't be surprised if her attacker knew exactly where she was.

Holly said, "My son, Daniel, is sleeping in the back room. I just want to check on him real quick."

"Sure."

Abby sipped the warm cocoa and gave a satisfied sigh. The store was very cute, with a lot of charm and personality. It felt cozy…safe.

A feeling she hadn't been familiar with for quite a while now. But she didn't let that lull her into dropping her guard. She glanced through the window to the mostly empty street beyond. The weather kept most people at home. Only the most hardy ventured out.

Soon Holly returned and sat opposite Abby. "I love being able to bring him to work with me."

The glowing eyes and bright smile told Abby that this was a woman who'd found contentment in her life.

"How did you get here through the snow and ice?"

Holly grinned. "Eli has to make it into work no matter what most days in the winter. He never knows what's going to happen or where. We have a snow plow. It's slow going, especially on the mountain roads, but we take our time and can generally get to where we need to go."

Abby smiled. "You love your life, don't you?"

"Every bit of it."

Envy surged back to the surface, this time for a different reason. Abby had lived her entire life in the shadow of her older sister. Keira had been the popular girl. She'd been cheerleader, prom queen and college valedictorian.

A restlessness to prove herself had led Abby to med school. A love for children made her choose obstetrics. She could understand Holly's delight in being able to bring her son to work and enjoy the simple mountain life.

"It'll still be pretty busy today in spite of the weather.

A lot of people live nearby and are able to walk to work. If someone else comes in, I'll have to pop up and help them."

"It's no problem." Her gaze took in a side room that held three computers. "What's that?"

Holly giggled. "I thought going high-tech would be pretty cool. Welcome to Rose Mountain's internet café."

The door jingled and Holly gave Abby a wry smile. "Duty calls."

Abby tensed and checked out the person who entered. An older gentleman in a black overcoat. Not Reese. She forced a smile. "Do you mind if I use one of the computers?"

"Not at all. Help yourself."

Holly went to help the customer and Abby stood, pulling her flash drive from her pocket. Within seconds, she had settled herself in front of the computer.

Soon, she was up and running, remotely accessing her work computer, praying no one was in her office to notice. For the next little while, she compared the data on her flash drive with the data on her computer.

Digging deep into her memory, she flagged information she thought had been altered. She kept an eye out for tests she hadn't ordered, injections she hadn't prescribed.

A shadow passed by the windows and she shivered.

Turning her attention back to the screen in front of her, she navigated her way into the area she'd studied about a week after sister's death.

She'd spent hours in the office, dulling her pain with mind-numbing work. Catching up on files, even entering patient data and insurance information.

When she came across Leticia Monroe's file, she paused, puzzled. According to this file, Leticia was labeled high risk and her insurance had been billed for tests Abby had never ordered.

She clicked on another patient record. Also billed for high-risk pregnancy, but this one was accurate.

Had Leticia's just been a mistake? She started opening the files of her other patients, going through each one, reading the information she'd written, orders she'd made, medication she'd prescribed.

Wait a minute. This wasn't right. Something was off. Several patients had drugs prescribed, expensive ones, that she rarely used. Abby sat back with a huff and stared at the screen. Had Reese somehow managed to do this? To access patient records and change them? As a police officer would he be able to do that?

Maybe.

Not by any ethical means, of course, but…

A chill invaded her body. Was he setting her up to take a fall of mammoth proportions?

The sound of a toddler crying jerked her attention from the screen. She looked up to see Holly hurrying toward the back room.

Daniel.

Her heart thudded in her chest. She realized she'd flashed back to the day at Fiona's apartment where she'd heard the crying baby only to have someone try to kidnap her.

She shuddered and went back to the computer.

In her search so far, Leticia's file was the only obvious aberration. The patient she remembered the most and knew she hadn't ordered that specific test. They wouldn't have needed it.

She clicked on the next one. This time, she didn't recognize the name. Sally Jensen.

"Who is she?"

"Who is who?" Holly asked from the door.

Abby jumped and swiveled her head toward Holly who stood in the doorway. Daniel blinked at her sleepily and Abby felt her heart constrict. "Oh, sorry. Talking to myself."

"Find something interesting?"

Abby's stomach clenched. She was dying to continue reading, but certainly didn't want to be rude to the sweet woman letting her hang out in the store. Abby forced a light laugh. "Not really." She changed the subject. "Is this Daniel?"

"Yes, can you say hi, Daniel?"

Daniel buried his face in his mother's shoulder, but peeked at Abby and offered her a grin. She smiled. "I can see why you lost your heart to that one. He's precious."

"Thank you."

Abby asked, "Did you get all your customers taken care of?"

"For now." Holly switched Daniel to her other hip. "I just need to feed this little guy before it gets even busier as the lunch crowd filters in."

Abby felt compelled to ask, "Is there anything I can do to help?"

Holly smiled. "No, I have a teenage helper, Tori Leigh, who comes in to watch Daniel during the busy time." She glanced at her watch. "In fact, she should be here any moment." Holly asked, "Would you like something to eat?"

Abby's stomach protested the thought of food. She was too tied up in knots to eat. "Maybe later, thanks."

The bell on the door rang out another greeting, and Holly nodded. "That's Tori now."

"I'm just going to finish what I was doing, if that's all right." Abby's fingers itched to keep clicking.

"Sure thing. And please don't think I'm rude if I don't speak over the next hour or so. Although, if you get hungry, just holler."

Holly went back to her business.

And Abby returned to her screen. Click, scroll, read, flag. Click, scroll, read. She fell into a pattern as she accessed each patient record.

About halfway through, she stopped and went back to Sally Jensen. Who was she? A new patient Abby had just forgotten about? A patient who belonged to one of her partners and she'd just been mislabeled under Abby's name?

Possibly.

She looked up to give her eyes a rest and they landed on little Daniel stuffing a piece of chicken into his mouth. He chomped happily while Tori Leigh played peekaboo with him.

Abby's heart stung. She wanted children. Wanted a family to call her own. Wanted everything her sister had had.

And lost.

The grief pinched, but she didn't look away from the happy child. She noticed Holly glancing at the duo every once in a while, and when her gaze would land on Daniel, her eyes would soften and her contentment would shine through.

Maybe one day, Abby sighed. Maybe God would allow that to happen for her. She turned back to the computer.

But for now, she couldn't think about relationships, love or babies until she figured out a way to get Reese off her case. Although thinking about relationships, love and babies brought Cal McIvers to the forefront of her mind. Abby gulped at the thought of spending the rest of her life with him. As his wife. The mother of his children.

Longing stabbed her, and she nearly gasped out loud at how bad she realized she wanted that.

But she couldn't have it.

Not yet. She needed to come clean and be completely honest with him about her role in her sister's death.

She frowned at the screen and forced her thoughts to focus. Sally Jensen. No, the name just didn't ring any bells. She decided to jot some notes, but before she could reach for her bag to grab a pen and paper, a cry echoed through the restaurant.

Abby jerked her head up to see a panicked Tori pounding on little Daniel's back. The baby's face was red, his little mouth open like a fish.

Instantly Abby stood and rushed over just as Holly reached for the choking toddler. "Daniel!"

A blue tinge circled his lips.

Abby said, "Give him to me."

Holly's terrified gaze slammed into hers and Abby could see the question there even as Holly took over pounding on the little guy's back.

Abby grabbed a chair and said the one thing that might make the woman trust her. "Give him to me. I'm a doctor."

Holly started, then handed over her precious child even as indecision warred on her face. Abby acted with quick, smooth movements. She sat and placed Daniel facedown over her thighs with his upper torso hanging over the side of her knee.

Using the heel of her hand, she thumped Daniel between the shoulder blades once, twice, three times.

The small piece of chicken landed on the floor and Daniel pulled in a gasping breath.

Then screamed an angry cry. "Mama!"

Abby nearly wilted with relief as Holly snatched him from her. Tears tracked down the mother's cheeks as she hugged her son whose cries had died down to whimpers.

"Thank you," Holly whispered to Abby. "Thank you. Thank you."

Tori added her own tearful gratitude and Abby finally noticed the small crowd staring at them. She flushed as one person started clapping and the rest joined in.

Anxious to escape the limelight, she smiled at Holly, ignored the burning questions she could see in the woman's eyes and hurried back to her computer.

Ducking her head, she tried to forget about the past few minutes and focus on figuring out who Sally Jensen was.

Abby bent over and began rummaging through her bag for a pen. She wanted to write the number down to call.

She heard someone settle in the desk beside her.

A black-gloved hand came into view and snatched the bag from her startled fingers. A hard shove sent her tumbling and she lost her balance to hit the floor. Startled, fear flowing, she looked up to see a hoodie-covered figure headed for the emergency exit.

A scream lodged in her throat as the thief burst through the door into the back alley.

The alarm screeched and customers careened their necks to see.

"I saw him," someone said. "He just grabbed her bag and ran out the door!"

Another voice hollered, "Someone call 9-1-1!"

Furious, Abby scrambled to her feet and shot out the door after the man. Terrified, she swallowed her fear and determined to put an end to this craziness once and for all.

NINE

Cal's radio squawked and he grabbed the microphone. "This is Alpha 304, go ahead."

"Disturbance at The Candy Caper reported. A thief snatched a bag and ran out the back through the emergency exit."

The Candy Caper? Alarm shot through Cal as he gunned the police cruiser in that direction. The chains on the tires gripped and held, allowing him fairly good traction. Snow swirled and his wipers were almost no match for the huge flakes now splashing onto his windshield.

He'd thought Abby would be safe at the store. And instead, he'd placed her right back in danger. Possibly. He didn't know that it was her bag that had been stolen.

But the feeling in his gut said it was.

With a twist of his wrist, he turned into the parking lot just to find customers standing, shielding their eyes from snow, necks craning to see…what?

Cal got out of the car, his gaze taking in every detail. "Holly? Abby? Where are you?"

He couldn't see either woman.

"Hey, Cal, that woman chased that guy down the street and behind the bank," Arthur James said.

Cal took off in the direction of the bank, calling for backup as he ran through the blinding snow.

"Cal!" Holly's voice.

He spun, slid, almost went down. "What?"

"It's Abby!"

He took off again. Somehow, he already knew that.

A loud crack echoed through the air and his heart dropped far enough for him to step on as he recognized the sound of a gunshot.

Abby froze as the bullet slammed into the building beside her spraying her with cement fragments. She ducked, making herself as small as possible against the side of the building. She forced herself to pull in slower breaths. Her thumping heart threatened to jump right out of her chest.

With terror and rage, she watched the hoodie-covered thief duck around the next building and disappear.

She let him go.

He'd shot at her.

What was she doing?

"What do you think you're doing?"

Abby straightened as though yanked by a string to stare into Cal's stormy blue eyes. Only they were more gray than blue as they drilled lasers into her. "Are you okay? I heard a shot. Nearly gave me a heart attack"

With a shaking finger, she pointed to the dent in the wall. "He missed me."

"Where'd he go?"

She pointed to the footprints in the snow. Footprints quickly being covered as more snow fell. Cal called it in, asking for all available officers to converge on the scene.

"He stole my bag." Her voice hitched and she wanted

to burst into tears. But she held on, refusing to give in to them. "And now he's getting away. You have to follow him." She gulped. "No, don't follow him. He has a gun."

"I'm not going to follow him." And she knew that he wouldn't give chase because she was here. "Come on." He grabbed her hand. "I don't want to be back here. We're sitting ducks and I didn't hear a car drive away."

Abby shook her head. "There's plenty of places around here to hide," she muttered.

Cal led her from the back of the building, keeping her behind him, his weapon drawn in front of him. She watched him in action and realized she felt completely safe in his presence. The feeling startled her. Warmed her.

Scared her.

Because it meant she should tell him everything.

They made it back to The Candy Caper where Holly waited, Daniel still clutched in her arms. When the woman saw them, she rushed from the still-lingering crowd. "Are you two okay?"

A tight-lipped Cal nodded. "Yes." Then he looked at Abby. "Are you crazy? Chasing after that guy?" His mild tone telling her more about his state of mind than if he'd started yelling at her. He was mad. Real mad.

Seeing things through his eyes, she could understand that. She ducked her head and shivered. She felt the cold seeping into her bones. "Probably." Then raised her gaze to meet his. "But he just made me so mad that I didn't even think of the consequences of chasing him. I just… did it."

Cal sighed and Holly motioned them inside. "At least it's warm in here." Eli came out of the back room where she'd been sitting when her bag was stolen. He tucked a small black notebook into his front pocket and clicked the pen in his left hand.

He looked at Cal and asked, "You figure out where he went? I've got Joel and Mitchell looking all over the area for him."

Cal shook his head. "By the time I caught up with Abby, he was gone and the snow was covering his tracks. But he's got a gun and isn't afraid to use it. The bullet's lodged in the wall near the fire escape behind the bank. I didn't take the time to dig it out as I wanted to get Abby away from there as fast as possible."

"I'll get Joel out there to collect it."

While he got on his radio to issue the request to Joel, Holly looked at Abby. "What were you thinking taking off after him?" Her southern accent was a little stronger than it had been a short time ago. She looked scared but determined not to show it.

Abby knew exactly how she felt. "It was stupid. I'm sorry."

Eli came back and looked at Abby. Then in a sudden movement, reached out and drew her into a hug under Cal's startled gaze. When he let her go, his throat worked and Abby knew he was trying to thank her. Holly must have had time to tell him about Daniel. She placed a hand on his arm and said, "It's all right."

"What's going on?" Cal asked, puzzlement plain in his face.

"Abby's a doctor. She saved Daniel's life," Holly said with a shudder. "He was choking on a piece of chicken and…if she hadn't been here…" Tears formed, but the mother managed to hold them back.

Abby felt embarrassed all over again. She smiled. "It's all right. I'm glad I was able to help."

Cal's gaze ping-ponged from one to the next, then

back. He looked like he wanted to say something but was at a loss for words. "A doctor?" He blinked then nailed her with a look that said they'd be talking later.

A few customers had returned to their food. Others stood at the big front windows trying to see if anything else exciting would happen.

Abby prayed there would be nothing more to see.

Another Rose Mountain police cruiser sat outside the store while the officer continued to question the occupants.

The door opened and a tall, rugged-looking man came in. He wore his deputy uniform confidently. She figured he wasn't a rookie and that made her feel good.

Eli looked up at him. "Joel, anything?"

"Nothing. We were able to follow the tracks a bit until the snow obliterated them. He must have run quite a ways. Probably had a car waiting, hopped in and took off."

"I never heard an engine start," Cal said.

Eli shook his head. "Might not get very far in this weather if he did, though." To Joel, he asked, "You get that bullet?"

Joel shook his head and held up a digital camera. "Found the hole it left, though."

Cal frowned and stepped forward. "What?"

"I think your man came back and dug out the bullet."

"Seriously?" Abby stared at the picture. The bullet was gone.

Eli blew out a breath and looked at Cal. "Explains why you didn't hear a car. I'm thinking we need to see who all is staying in town at the Rose Mountain Inn."

Cal shrugged. "Worth a try I suppose. Lots of visitors this time of year. We've got only another week until

Christmas and we can't do a background check on everyone."

Eli scowled. "I know that."

"He might not be staying in a hotel here anyway. Could be sleeping in his car or camping out."

"Mighty cold," Eli mused.

"It's still doable," Cal argued.

Joel said, "Well, wherever he is, he's probably going to sit tight for a while. He got what he was after."

"Yeah, my bag." Abby gritted her teeth wondering once again what Reese would have to gain stealing her bag. Was it just one more way to assert his power over her? Was he doing his best to make her suffer before he got his hands on her? Probably.

Cal looked at Abby. "Did you get a good look at him?"

"No. He had his face covered. He was wearing one of those hoodie sweatshirts. All I saw was the floor and the back of him as he raced out."

Cal turned to Eli and Holly. "Are there any security cameras?"

"Yes," Eli nodded. "We'll get the footage and take a look."

"In the meantime, I suggest you get Abby back to the ranch if that's where she's going. The roads are getting bad. If anything develops, I'll give you a call."

After Abby thanked Holly for her hospitality, Cal ushered her out to the car. "I've got to stop by the office and pick up my truck. There's no way I'm driving this thing home."

They crept through the still-falling snow and Abby hunched in the passenger seat pondering the latest incident. She was going to have to tell Cal about Reese. Convince Cal to help her get Reese off her back. All she wanted was to be alone and try to find a measure of peace.

And the only way she was going to have any peace is if she turned around and faced God instead of trying to outrun Him.

She had to admit that life on the run wasn't for her. Part of her wanted to give up, face Reese and beg his forgiveness one more time. But she just wasn't ready to face his rejection, his contempt.

And she'd tried that before.

She'd approached him at church, tried to talk to him and he'd brushed her off without a word. Just gave her a look so chilling she still hadn't thawed out.

"Are you okay?"

With a start, she realized Cal had parked the car next to the SUV and was waiting for her to move. "Oh. Sorry. I was thinking."

His eyes smiled at her. "I could tell. What about?"

She sighed. "Forgiveness. And why it's so hard to give sometimes."

A scowl chased away his smile. "I know."

Abby studied him. "Who do you need to forgive?"

"Come on. Let's get in the truck."

So he didn't want to talk about it. She could understand that.

They transferred themselves to the other vehicle, Abby's fingers touching the little pouch she'd sewn into her jeans. Comfort filled her when her hand felt the money, the ID and cell phone. She'd almost thrown them into her bag and had decided at the last minute to stick them in the little pocket.

Maybe God was looking out for her after all. She looked at the strong man in the seat beside her. He believed in forgiveness, he believed in God. Maybe…

"His name's Mark Sawls."

His deep voice came out of nowhere and Abby focused on him. "What?"

"You asked who I needed to forgive. I need to forgive Mark Sawls, Brianne's husband, for killing her."

Abby's sharp gasp echoed in the cab of the truck. "I'm so sorry."

"I am, too." His jaw flexed and his fingers gripped the wheel. "She went to Fiona and told her she felt like her husband was losing it. He was a fellow cop. He came from a larger city, had dealt with the kind of crimes we don't really see around here. One of them involved the death of a teen killed by his mother. She shot him in his sleep."

Abby winced. "That's awful."

"It seemed to haunt Mark, but none of us knew how bad it was. Brianne got pregnant in high school at the age of sixteen. Mark was crazy about her and married her when her son, Isaac, was two. Apparently Isaac was causing a lot of problems at home. He was twelve and there was a lot of friction between him and Brianne. I never saw that it was anything more than typical preteen rebellion. Mark saw it as something more, I guess."

"What happened?" she whispered.

Cal rubbed a hand across his eyes briefly before narrowing them back on the road. "Brianne came to Fiona several times. Not only were they cousins, but they were also best friends who'd grown up together, were roommates in college and then moved back home after graduation. They even taught at the same school." He cleared his throat. "Brianne had bruises all the time. She finally came to Fiona and told her she wanted to leave Mark, but was afraid she'd lose her son if she did. Mark had adopted him when they got married and Isaac seemed to prefer Mark over his mother."

"What a choice." She paused. "No, there was no choice for her, was there? She had to stay or lose her son completely."

Cal shook his head. "Fiona came to me, begged me to help."

"What did you do?"

"I went to Mark and asked him about it. He got really sad, even had tears in his eyes. He said Brianne had been talking crazy. She'd run into something, get a bruise and accuse him of hitting her. He said he tried to get her help, but she just wouldn't listen and he was at his wit's end."

"And you believed him." A chill covered her.

"Yes." Cal's sigh spoke volumes. "I believed him."

"Because he was a fellow cop." Abby bit her lip and looked out the window. A low-slung car followed a safe distance behind. Absently she noted the chains on the tires, watched them roll and cut through the tracks Cal's vehicle left behind.

"Yes, partly. But because he was so convincing. I'd never seen him like that before. He was torn up. And even Fiona had said Brianne was distraught, depressed and acting a little strange."

"Because she was a victim in her own home. She didn't feel safe. She was trying to survive even as she tried to figure out what to do." Abby knew it as well as she knew her own name.

"Yeah, I guess. But none of us saw it that way."

"Because the cop, her husband, said so." She couldn't help the bitterness that stung her words.

"And it's one of the reasons I've never been able to let it go." Cal glanced at her and she shivered at the pain centered in his eyes. When he looked back to the road, Abby felt a small stirring of hope. Had he learned his lesson? Would he believe her if she told him about Reese? Believe that she hadn't done anything wrong— legally—and if Reese or someone he hired was after her, that he was out to hurt her?

Maybe.

But what would he say about the fact that she'd filed a restraining order against a cop? How would he feel about that?

She wasn't sure she wanted to know.

"You saved Daniel's life." His statement came out of nowhere.

"He was choking. I simply cleared his airway." She noticed the car again. It seemed out of place on this lonely stretch between town and Cal's ranch. Cal's eyes flicked to the rearview mirror and she saw his brows draw down toward the bridge of his nose. Eyes still on the mirror, he said, "Holly said you're a doctor."

Abby paused. "Yes."

"Why didn't you share this little bit of information about yourself before?"

She sighed. "Because it wasn't important. It doesn't define who I am. Right now, I'm not Dr. O'Sullivan. I'm Abby. Just a woman trying to make sense out of a life gone crazy," she finished on a whisper.

She felt his fingers grip hers for a brief moment and knew he'd accepted her need to be a woman. Not a doctor.

"But you still helped Daniel."

"Of course I did." She frowned. "Just because I don't want to be a doctor right now doesn't mean I can just set aside those skills when someone's in an emergency situation."

"I didn't mean to imply— Get down!"

The back windshield exploded as Cal jerked her down and toward him. He yanked the wheel to the left at the same time. Abby's scream echoed through the SUV.

The heavy vehicle bounced off the main road. Cal kept his foot off the brake and let the vehicle bump along. His gaze swept behind him as the cold air blew in from the back.

Abby shot up and spun around to look out. "He's still there."

Cal grabbed her coat and yanked her back down. "And he probably still has a gun, so stay out of sight."

The SUV came to a stop, and Cal released his own weapon from his holster. With one eye on the vehicle still sitting on the road, he grabbed his cell phone and punched in Eli's number.

When the man answered, Cal hollered, "Someone just shot out the back of my truck. I need some backup."

"Shot out—" Eli sputtered, then growled, "Where are you?"

Another shot cracked the driver's side mirror and Cal flinched as Eli shouted, "Was that another shot?"

"Yes," Cal shouted back. "We're sitting ducks, Eli."

He scanned the trees ahead. The ranch lay in that direction, but did they dare leave what little protection the car offered to hike through the trees?

He looked at her white pinched face and felt the anger surge through him. Fingers wrapped around the 9mm, Cal watched the man in the vehicle, taking in as many details as he could.

The business end of a rifle stared back at him. With the tinted window only partially lowered, Cal couldn't get a good look at the driver. Keeping his head low, he asked Abby, "You know anyone who drives an older model gray Buick?"

"No."

"Me, neither." From his position, Cal saw the Buick roll forward, then stop again.

What was he doing?

Head low, Cal pressed the gas to the SUV. The chains grabbed and held and the vehicle inched forward. Another crack sounded a bullet slammed into the back.

Abby gave another whimper. "I'm so sorry," she whispered and Cal's anger mounted.

"It's not your fault. You didn't ask for this." Teeth gritted, he said, "Eli will be here as soon as possible."

"It's not going to be soon enough. What is he waiting on?"

Her question echoed his own. "I don't know."

Again, he pressed the gas pedal and again the SUV moved forward.

The Buick backed up. Slowly. Inch by inch. Then the rifle fixated on the driver's side of the SUV.

"Duck!" Cal grabbed Abby head and pulled her down to shelter her beneath his own body. Tremors shivered through her and he could almost taste her fear.

The driver's window shattered, raining glass over them. Cal flinched as the small pieces stung the back of his neck.

He looked up and around.

The Buick's taillights were fading.

But was the guy leaving? Or just making him think he was?

Cal grabbed Abby's hand. "Come on, we're going to hike it to my house."

"Hike? I don't even know if I can stand up right now."

Shock had bleached her face of any color she might have started the day with.

"You have a determined psycho on your tail. He's already attacked you twice today. I don't know if he's gone or coming back. We need to get out of the car while we can and get to some stable shelter." Like his house where he had weapons and enough ammo to outlast their attacker.

The hum of an engine reached his ears.

Abby's stricken gaze slammed into his.

Opening his door, he rolled out of the vehicle, glass falling from him to land in the snow. He heard Abby open her door and soon she was beside him.

Grabbing her hand, he pulled her toward the trees and in the direction of his house.

Heart in her throat, Abby stumbled along beside Cal, risking a glance over her shoulder. She had no idea where they were or where he was taking her.

But she had to trust that he knew what he was doing.

Her legs shook so badly that she wondered if she could make it to wherever he was leading her. She hadn't been kidding when she'd told him she wasn't sure she could stand.

So far, she was holding her own.

"Where are we going?"

"My house. It's just over that hill. The trees will hide us pretty well. At least until we come to my backyard."

With his left hand, his fingers gripped hers. With his right, he held his weapon ready.

"Was that him coming back? The engine we heard?" Abby gasped in air as she hurried beside him. The cold stung her cheeks and she wished she had grabbed her gloves from the dash.

"I don't know. Either him or Eli. I'm hoping Eli, expecting the bad guy, you know?"

"Oh." And then she had no more breath for talking. She struggled through the snow, slipping occasionally, grateful for Cal's steady hand.

And then they came to the edge of the trees. About half a football field's length away, Cal's house sat on a gentle slope.

It reminded her of a cozy log cabin and she couldn't wait to get there.

But first they had to get across the open expanse of white.

Abby caught her breath and watched him scan the area. He was on the phone with Eli again. When he hung up, he said, "Eli said he found my SUV."

"But not the Buick?"

"Nope. Eli's put out a BOLO for the Buick. Right now, he's going to see if a tow truck can get in and he can get the SUV towed to a repair shop for me. He's got everyone on duty looking for the Buick, Abby, we'll find it—and the guy who goes with it."

She shivered and saw his eyes dart one way, then back. "We're going to make a run for it, okay?"

"You think he's waiting for us?"

Cal's tight jaw got tighter. "I don't know. But I can't leave you here alone to go find out."

She agreed with that. The last thing she wanted was to be left behind.

Cal still held his phone and she heard it vibrate. He held it to his ear. "Hello?" Pause. "Where? Okay, I'll be on the lookout."

"What?" she asked, fear nearly choking her.

"Joel came across the Buick. It's empty and belongs to Steve Jacobs. He reported it stolen this morning."

"And no sign of the guy who tried to kill us?"

"Eli's asking CSU to come in and process it."

Abby noticed that even as he talked, he never took his eyes from their surroundings, his hyperalertness never dissipated.

"Okay," he said, "come on."

With a firm grip on her hand, he pulled her away from the shelter of the trees. They hurried, slogging their way through the snow toward Cal's front door.

Abby noticed that he kept her back to his front and knew that he was doing his best to make sure she was as small a target as possible.

Just before they hit the front porch, Cal let go of her hand. When she heard the jingle of keys, she figured out why. He didn't lose a step jamming it into the lock and turning it.

Throwing the door open, he pushed her in and slammed the dead bolt home after him. Abby's legs gave out and she sank to the floor. Cal looked at her. "You okay?"

"I will be." Maybe.

"Be right back."

From her position by the front door, she watched him stride through the foyer and into the kitchen. Then he turned right and disappeared from her view, not worried about the snow he was tracking along his wood floors.

Looking around, it dawned on her that she was in Cal's house. A beautiful log house with a green roof. The stone fireplace awaited a match. Murmuring came to her and she realized he was on the phone with someone again.

Heavy boots announcing his return distracted her from her perusal.

When he saw her still sitting where he'd left her, he

raised a brow. "I called Joseph and Fiona and told them to be on guard. Joseph's contacting the rest of the men. If this guy shows up, we'll be ready and waiting for him."

Abby bit her lip as he held out a hand to help her up. She reached for him and when his warm fingers closed around hers she wanted to burst into tears or fling herself into his arms.

Then she took note of the rifle in his other hand. "What are you going to do?"

"Go hunting."

TEN

Joseph's truck sat in the drive as Cal escorted her back to his sister's house. "What's Joseph going to say about me coming back here?"

"I talked to him. He's okay with it."

He sounded sure, but Abby had her doubts. For now, she didn't have a choice. She was stuck. On a ranch with at least one person who didn't want her here. A pregnant woman who might deliver any day in the middle of a snowy winter.

And a person who seemed determined to cause her enormous amounts of grief.

She couldn't help but wonder how Cal's mother felt about her. Probably the same way her own mother felt. According to Abby's mother, Abby had betrayed them, her mother, her sister, Reese…all of them. And she didn't deserve their love anymore. Or their forgiveness.

Maybe that's why she felt God had turned His back on her, too. If the people who were supposed to love her the most could do that to her, why wouldn't God?

The very idea shook her faith to the core.

But God was perfect. Humans were…human.

Then she didn't have time to think anymore as Cal helped her out of the truck.

"It stopped snowing." A winter wonderland of beautiful, endless white greeted her.

"Yep, but it'll start back up again, I'm sure."

Smoke rose from the bunkhouse chimney and she knew the men must have decided to get out of the weather.

All in all, it looked like peace reigned out here.

She looked at the house and walked toward it.

And braced herself for the reception she was afraid she was going to receive.

She shouldn't have wasted her energy worrying.

Fiona threw her arms around her as soon as Abby stepped inside. "Oh, I'm so glad you came back." Joseph stood with his arms crossed, his hostility level only slightly decreased from when he'd dropped her at the bus station.

Wrapped in the woman's awkward embrace, Abby felt something nudge her belly. Then a more forceful punch made her gasp a laugh. Pulling back she fought the tears. How many times had Keira called her over to feel the baby move?

Fiona giggled. "Sorry, not even born yet and I can't control him."

"Her," Joseph muttered. He straightened and looked at Abby. "Cal says you're okay." His expression softened. "If Cal says he trusts you, then I do, too. You're welcome to the basement apartment."

"Thanks, Joseph."

"Besides, Cal said you're a doctor." He eyed Fiona's round figure. "A doctor might come in handy in the next few days."

He could have said anything but that and she would have been fine. Now terror struck her heart. There was no way she was delivering that baby in this house. "But you said you could get her to the hospital no matter the weather."

"Sure, that's the plan and I have the vehicle to do it, but it sure is comforting to know you're here."

For the first time since her sister's death, Abby felt the need to be closer to God, to pray and have her prayers answered. *Please, God, don't ask me to deliver that baby.*

But the uneasy feeling in her gut said God might have other plans for her.

She cast a wary glance at Cal and the sympathy on his face made her feel only marginally better. Forcing a smile, she said, "Well, now that my bag was stolen and shopping is out of the question, I might need to borrow a few items of clothing."

Fiona laughed and side-hugged her. "No problem."

Thursday morning, Cal shook his head and looked at Joseph. "Temperature's dropping. We need to get those horses in the barn. You ready to round 'em up?"

"Ready when you are."

"Jesse and the boys are already bringing them in."

Joseph looked at the sky. "At least the snow's slowed down."

"For now. It's supposed to start up again later tomorrow. But it's supposed to be in the teens tonight. We're going to have us one big ice-skating rink." Cal pressed his lips together and thought about his sister. They'd all assured her that they'd get her to the hospital as soon as she gave them the word. But that was in a normal snowy winter. Not this icy stuff that was expected.

He looked at Joseph. "I think we should get Fiona into town. At least where Dylan can get to her to help deliver the baby. I know we told her it was no big deal to get her to the hospital, but I gotta be honest, I'm worried."

His brother-in-law frowned and looked at the sky. "You might be right."

"I think we can still get her there. Driving home earlier wasn't so bad with the chains on the tires, but after this stuff turns to ice—" He pulled in a deep breath. "Yeah, not so sure about that."

His thoughts turned to the man who'd stolen Abby's bag. Where was he? Was he camping out somewhere on the land, waiting for his next chance at Abby or was he snugged up in a hotel room biding his time, waiting for the storm to pass?

He just didn't know. Which meant he and his men couldn't drop their guard for a minute.

As he and Joseph headed out to the pasture, his phone rang. "Hello?"

"Cal, it's Eli. I looked at the video footage from Holly's store."

"You get anything?" Anticipation churned inside him. If they could get a positive ID on the guy, they'd be able to find him.

"Not much." Eli's disgusted sigh deflated Cal's hope. "We got that he's about five-ten to six feet and even though the video's black-and-white, it looks like the guy has light-colored hair."

"Could you see his face?"

"No. He was careful to keep the hoodie pulled over it." Eli paused. "It looks like he slipped into the store during the commotion with Daniel. He never once looked away from Abby. When she went back into the internet area, this guy followed her, gave her a shove and grabbed her bag."

Cal grimaced. "All right. Thanks for the update. I'll pass the description on to the guys. We'll be on the lookout."

Back in the small apartment, Abby rubbed her chilled arms, did her best to put the two latest attempts on her life out of her head and stared at the computer screen.

Insurance fraud.

She'd finally figured it out. It was the only thing that made sense. But who was responsible for it?

Fortunately, she had access to all of her partners' files. Sometimes they shared patients, so they had to be able to access it to make notes, update information or whatever.

But how would she be able to tell who was actually responsible for the fraud? It would take someone more computer savvy than herself. She wondered if a computer-forensics person would be able to track the original source.

In actuality, it looked like the blame lay on her shoulders. She gulped. Was someone setting her up? So that she would take the fall if the fraud was ever discovered?

A sick feeling invaded her. Who would do this? And why? Well, for the money obviously, but as to the who...

It would almost have to be one of her partners, wouldn't it? Or one of the office staff who had access. She thought about Lisa, one of the secretaries, who always seemed to find an excuse to be in Abby's office. Or the receptionist who stayed late to "just finish up."

Abby gave up going through the list of employees. It was too long.

She'd have to check each and every file. Then again, while she knew her regular patients well, she wouldn't know the others who she didn't see on a regular basis.

Abby sat back in the chair with a huff. So, what now? She needed to make a phone call.

But how could she do it without the call being traced? Then again, did taking precautions really matter? It was obvious whoever was after her knew exactly where she was. Which was why she should have kept going or at least stayed in the bus station. If Reese brought grief to this little family...

Standing, she grabbed her jeans from the chair where she'd tossed them before slipping into a pair of Fiona's sweats. Reaching into the little hideaway pocket, she pulled out the cell phone and battery. She slipped the battery into the back of the phone and powered it up.

Twenty missed calls.

She scrolled through her call list.

None from her parents. Tears stung the back of her eyelids and she blinked. Then noticed one particular call that caught her attention. An outgoing call to her mother made—after she'd been here with the McIvers.

Someone had used her phone to call her mother.

Cal.

He'd been snooping through the apartment, found her phone and...made the call.

It had to have been him.

A sense of betrayal rushed through her. Then she stopped. Could she blame him? He hadn't known her at all when he'd brought her into his home. Of course it made sense that he would check up on her.

Abby stilled, her fingers remained wrapped around the phone. Cal hadn't even asked her about her last name being O'Sullivan when he read the letter.

Because he'd already known it.

He'd talked to one of her parents. Probably her mother because that was the number he'd called.

Sorrow hit her and she wanted to weep. He hadn't told her he'd called her mother most likely because her mother didn't want anything to do with Abby. And Cal was trying to spare her. Possibly. Or gather more evidence against her.

"Lord, please," she whispered the anguished prayer. "Please let them forgive me one day."

On the phone, Cal spoke to Jesse. They'd already made three trips, horses in tow. The whole process was taking longer than usual because Cal wanted everyone to work in teams. One to gather the horses and one to keep a watch on the surrounding area for anyone who wanted to get trigger-happy.

The barns held forty-two stalls in all, thirty-one of them in use.

Joseph led two horses. Cal brought up the rear with the last three. He was cold and wanted a warm cup of coffee and some time with Abby. The thought of her waiting at the house made his stomach clench in anticipation.

His heart thudded and he just shook his head at the emotions roiling through him.

He'd almost lost her, though. When she'd insisted on leaving, he'd wanted to grab her and hold her so she couldn't escape. So she wouldn't *want* to leave.

"You okay?" Joseph asked.

"Yep. Just thinking."

"About a pretty little redhead?"

Cal smiled. "Something like that."

The teasing light in Joseph's eyes died as he slid from the back of his horse and looped the reins over the rail in front of the barn. He did the same with one of the other horses. "You be careful with her, Cal. We don't know much about her."

Defensiveness rose in him and then fizzed. Joseph was right. "I know. I asked Eli to do a background check on her after I read that letter."

Relief lit up his brother-in-law's face. "What did he find out?"

"Haven't heard anything from him yet, which means he didn't turn up anything." He wondered if he should tell Eli to make it a priority. "Watch the ice."

Joseph clicked and led the one horse into the barn, avoiding some icy patches where the snow had been packed down and frozen over.

Cal dismounted and looped his reins next to Joseph's horse who tossed his head. Cal patted his neck and turned his attention to the skittish mare next to him. Working with her had been difficult. She'd been neglected and malnourished by the time Leigh Ann, Joel's wife, had found her.

Determined to rescue the horse, Leigh Ann had decided Cal's ranch was the perfect place for the animal. Normally, he didn't take in horses that needed that much work, but Leigh Ann had begged him and he'd caved.

He had to admit she was doing much better, learning to trust human hands rather than fear them.

Cal led his horses into the barn, one by one and put them in their individual stalls. Joseph forked over the hay and made sure the water buckets were filled.

"Going to get Princess Mary," Joseph said as he rubbed Snickers's nose.

"I'll get her if you want to head on up to check on Fiona."

"Naw, it'll take only a minute."

Cal nodded and gave Snickers the apple he was

searching for. After giving Snickers one last pat, Cal headed out of the barn, Abby's pretty face at the forefront of his mind.

Joseph had his hands on the skittish horse's lead when a barn cat shot from the building right under Princess Mary's front hooves. The horse reared in fright and came down hard on the snow. Joseph stumbled and backed up, still holding the lead.

A loud crack sounded and puffed up ice and snow in front of Joseph and the horse.

Cal watched in disbelief as the horse reared again, only to come down, one shoed hoof catching Joseph in the shoulder spinning him into the hitching rail.

"Joseph!"

Cal started toward him as the man screamed his pain and went down. The mare went up on her hind legs for the third time, hit an icy patch and fell straight toward the already wounded man.

Cal froze. "Joseph! Roll!"

This time the scream came from the animal as she lost her balance, a high-pitched cry that scraped across Cal's nerves, sending waves of fear all over him.

Joseph made the attempt even as his eyes widened in terror to see the huge animal heading for him. His desperate move slid him farther from the horse, but not completely out of the way.

There was no way to move, no way to act fast enough to grab the horse or reach Joseph to pull him out of the way. All Cal could do was watch as the heavy animal's feet shot out from under her and crash, back first, on top of Joseph.

Joseph's keening cry ended abruptly and Cal's heart froze with grief and fury.

Someone had shot at them. The shocking realization registered, but his first priority was to rescue his brother-in-law.

Cal raced for the thrashing animal's head, desperate to pull her away from Joseph. Was he dead? Terror beat a swift beat in his chest. Prayers left his lips fast and furious.

Another scream sounded. This time human.

He didn't dare look up, but knew that Fiona stood in the doorway of the house, no doubt lured there by the commotion. "Get back inside!" he yelled at her.

He had no idea if she obeyed him or not. His fingers gripped the lead on the horse and pulled. The animal worked with him and soon Cal had the animal back on her feet, trembling, head hung low.

He cast a glance at Joseph who lay still, unconscious, face pale and gray, blood rushing from a gash on his head. His arm lay twisted at an odd angle.

Running footsteps sounded and he saw a flash of red hair as Abby dropped beside Joseph. Fiona was right behind her. His heart thudded in fear at their exposure.

"Someone shot at us," Cal ground out. "We've got to get him inside the barn."

"Shot at you?" Her eyes went wide as she spared him a shocked glance. Then her gaze dropped right back to the wounded man as she assessed his injuries. Fiona didn't seem to hear him as she clutched her husband's hand.

"We need to get him into cover. Now, move, move. Please." As much as he wanted to help Joseph, he had to make sure the horse wouldn't be able to hurt anyone else if another shot sounded.

"We can't move him yet, we might do more damage." Her hands ran expertly over Joseph's arms, his head, his neck...

Cal pulled the mare farther into the barn and looped her reins through one of the hooks on the wall. Jesse and Zane appeared, eyes on their wounded friend. "Help me get Joseph and the women in the barn. Someone's up in the hills shooting at us!" Cal hollered as he bolted back toward Joseph and Abby.

Abby looked up, her face tight, jaw clenched. "His arm is broken. I think the horse landed on it. I'll need materials to splint it."

"Fine." Cal's nerves itched up and down his spine. Did she not understand what he was saying? "Abby, we'll take care of it in there."

"I have to help him." She sounded almost frantic.

He grabbed her and Fiona and pulled them protesting toward cover. "You can't help him if you're dead."

Zane and Jesse lifted the man as carefully as possible. Joseph didn't even twitch although if he'd been awake, he'd have been in horrible pain.

Desperate fear tugged at Cal as he led Abby and Fiona to shelter. Prayers winged from his lips to God's ears as the men moved Joseph into the cover of the barn. As soon as they were in, Cal let go of the women and grabbed a blanket. He laid it on a pile of fresh hay.

The men placed Joseph on the blanket and stepped back.

Abby dropped beside Joseph and rattled off the items she needed. Zane said, "I'll get the stuff." He raced off to the house before Cal could protest the man making himself a target. He rushed to the door to see Zane make it safely inside.

Jesse grabbed his rifle. "I'm going hunting."

Cal looked at him. "No, there's not enough cover out there. You'll be an easy target."

Looking like he wanted to argue, Jesse nevertheless

clamped his lips shut and turned. "I'm going to find me a window to keep watch then. If he starts shooting again, at least I can shoot back."

Cal nodded and watched as Abby bent over Joseph, checking his eyes, his pulse. She leaned over and placed her ear on his chest. "No wheezing that I can hear, lungs sound good." She looked at Cal. "Can EMS get out here?"

He tossed his phone to Fiona. "Call 9-1-1. Tell them what they're coming into, that there's a shooter somewhere close by." But in his gut, he knew that if Joseph needed emergency care, it was going to be bad all around.

Abby must have been thinking the same thing. "Tell them we need a Life Flight helicopter. There's plenty of space for them to land out here. They'll have two nurses and everything on board for a patient in Joseph's condition. And most of them won't care if there's danger, they just want to get to the victim."

If they would be able to fly in this weather. He looked at the sky. Possibly. But it was the shooter on his land that worried him the most. Regardless of whether they'd be willing to take a chance on getting hit by a stray bullet, he wasn't willing to put them in that kind of danger on his land.

Zane made it back into the barn, arms laden with the items Abby needed. Jesse stood in the window, alert, rifle ready.

Tossing a glance in Jesse's direction, Cal told Zane, "We're going to have find the person who shot at us. If they could even make it, we can't expect EMS to come out here with a sniper on the loose and Joseph can't afford for them not to."

Zane nodded and grabbed a horse. "I'll find him or make sure he's gone."

"Tell Jesse to cover you. With the two of you watching each other's backs, you should be all right." He hoped.

A vehicle approached, chains crunching in the snow.

Cal looked out the door of the barn to see his mother pull up. He wasn't fast enough to stop her from getting out of the vehicle. He bolted out of the barn to wrap his large frame around her smaller one. With his other hand, he grabbed Tiffany. He practically carried the two of them to the shelter of the barn. The entire five seconds his back was exposed to the hills, he expected to feel a bullet slam into it.

ELEVEN

"Cal, what on earth are you doing?" his mother demanded as she pulled out of his hold. Tiffany struggled to get down. Then his mother's eyes landed on Joseph. "What happened?" Her horrified voice trembled through him.

Fiona gave a wailing cry, her fingers still clutched around the phone, and flew to her mother, wrapping her arms around the woman as best she could. "He's hurt bad, Mom. Someone shot at him and spooked the horse." She finished the tale and his mother immediately went to her son-in-law to feel his pulse and check him out for herself.

Cal dialed Eli's number and filled him in.

"Give me the vicinity where the shot came from," Eli demanded. Fortunately, the sheriff knew the McIvers property almost as well as his own. Cal told him. "Zane and Jesse are already up there, so tell the boys not to shoot unless they know what they're shooting at."

"They'll be careful." Cal heard the censure in Eli's voice. He was right. Cal had no cause to give such a reminder. The deputies were well-trained and beyond competent. Eli said, "Joel's already out near you. His

SUV can probably make it pretty quick. Mitchell might be a while."

"I need that helicopter able to land, Eli. Joseph might die if it doesn't." He kept his voice low, casting a glance in Fiona's direction.

"I hear you, buddy."

Cal hung up with another silent prayer. He walked to the back of the barn and unlocked the rifle case his father had built when Cal was just a boy. He pulled out his dad's Winchester rifle and a handful of bullets.

As Fiona gathered her composure, Cal turned to watch Abby continue her examination, hands moving expertly over Joseph, pushing his heavy jacket aside. "What can I do to help?" Cal demanded.

She paused at Joseph's stomach and pressed. Pressed again.

"Abby?"

"Shush."

She felt Joseph's pulse again. Listened to his chest. When she raised her eyes, she said, "We need him out of here now. I think he's got some internal bleeding going on in his abdomen."

Cal blinked in the face of Abby's competence. Mentally, he knew she was a doctor. Seeing her in action brought it home to him. She was a *doctor.* She'd help Joseph. Relief flowed over Cal. Joseph had medical care.

One by one his mother handed the splint items Jesse had placed next to Joseph over to Abby. She then scooted out of the way. Fiona had fallen silent, tears streaming down her cheeks as she watched Abby work on her husband.

Within minutes, Abby had the arm splinted.

She then returned her attention to Joseph's abdomen

area. She unbuttoned his flannel shirt and placed her hands on his stomach. Her lips tightened. "This area is rigid, tight. Look at his belly button."

Cal did. It looked to be a light shade of blue. "It's bruised?" His jaw tightened. "Internal bleeding?"

"Yes. It's called Cullen's sign," she whispered. "Which means he's definitely bleeding on the inside. If he's got Cullen's sign, his pancreas could be damaged—and who knows what else. He needs X-rays and surgery asap."

Worry clutched him by the throat and wouldn't let go. "Fiona, is EMS on the way?"

She looked at him and nodded. "I told them to send a helicopter. She said she would if one could get out." Fiona looked at the phone as though she'd never seen one before. "I'm still on the phone with her."

Abby shivered. "Okay, it's chilly in here, but I don't want to move him unless we just absolutely have to. Without X-rays, I don't know about anything else going on inside him, but we need to protect him against shock. His heavy coat is waterproof, that protected him a little from his fall in the snow. Now we need some blankets to cover him with."

"I'll get them," Cal's mother said. She hurried back into the tack room leaving Fiona looking lost and afraid but trying to be brave. Tiffany clutched her hand, her eyes wide and curious and a tad alarmed.

Cal's mother returned with an armload of blankets and Cal jumped up to take them from her. "Thanks, Mom."

Abby looked up at Fiona. "Are you all right? Any pains?"

Fiona placed a hand over her belly. "No, we're okay. I'm just worried about Joseph."

After what seemed like an eternity but was in reality probably only about twenty minutes of watching Joseph get worse and Abby's face get tighter, Cal finally heard the helicopter. Abby was right. The crew was willing to fly into the face of possible danger. Probably wasn't the first time for them.

Two minutes later, the chopper landed in the field behind the barn and Cal opened the barn's back door, eyes scanning the horizon, looking for any kind of movement or reflection of light. The bullet had come from the opposite side of the building, but he wasn't taking any chances. He had no guarantee the person hadn't changed locations.

One woman and one man dressed in uniforms hopped from the chopper. One grabbed a stretcher, the other, a red box.

They ran toward Cal, faces intense, ready to save a life. Cal held his rifle ready in case he needed to offer fire coverage.

He felt better already and offered a silent prayer of thanks to God for placing Abby in their lives.

Abby, the doctor.

He moved out of the way as the medical team hustled into the barn unscathed. And Abby started barking information. One of the paramedics raised a brow at her professional tone. She noticed and simply said, "I'm a doctor."

Soon, Joseph was hooked up to an IV, his vital signs being monitored by the minute and he was being carried toward the waiting helicopter.

"Wait!" Fiona cried. "I'm going, too."

At Fiona's cry, Abby looked up, ready to protest but the paramedic beat her to it. "Sorry, ma'am," he said, "there's no room. It's an older chopper. They'll barely have room to do what we need to do to keep your husband alive." And then he was gone, rushing to save Joseph's life.

Jesse, who had returned from the search empty-handed, wrapped an arm around Fiona's shoulders. "I'll drive you in."

Cal hustled out behind the medical team as they rushed Joseph to the waiting chopper. He held his rifle ready and Abby wanted to weep, to fall on her face and beg their forgiveness for bringing danger to their doorstep. But there was no time. Abby waved the chopper on and it took off in a rush of wind and the roar of the blades.

Cal raced back to the barn and slammed the door shut behind him.

"Which hospital are they taking him to?" Fiona cried.

"The one in Asheville," Cal said. "Mission Hospital."

"I've got to be with him." Then she grasped her stomach and gave a different sort of cry.

One of startled surprise.

Abby gasped as she watched the woman's face tighten, her breathing practically stopped. Fiona made no sound for several seconds, then she pulled in a deep breath.

"You just had a contraction, didn't you?" Abby asked.

Wide-eyed, Fiona nodded. "I think I did." Still wide-eyed, she said, "That hurt."

Concerned, terrified she'd sent the chopper off when she had another patient on her hands, Abby felt a wave of nausea rush over her.

Cal reached out and grasped his sister's arm. Jesse looked alarmed. "We need to drive her in?" he asked.

"It's too early for the baby," Fiona breathed.

"Babies make up their own minds about when they want to put in an appearance," Cal's mother warned.

Abby shivered, looked out the nearest window and noticed the darkening sky. The clouds rolled in and more snow threatened. "I think we need to drive Fiona in to the hospital while we can."

"No." Fiona's stubborn streak reared its head and Abby wanted to smack her. "It would be a different hospital than Joseph. I don't want that. Let's just wait and see." Fiona looked up at her brother. "Just help me get inside and lie down for a—" Her breath cut off again as her face scrunched with the pain of another contraction.

And Abby felt dread crawl up her spine as she glanced at her watch. Four minutes between the two contractions.

What she wouldn't give for some nefedipine. But Fiona didn't need the drug to stop her contractions. She was only two weeks from delivery. If she had the baby now, the little one would most likely be fine.

But Abby would rather she wait. She looked at Cal. "Is it safe to leave the barn and get to the house where she can lie down?"

Cal got on the phone. Abby heard him asking about the shooter. When he hung up, his lips pursed tight. Then he said, "They found where he was waiting, but he was gone by the time Zane got there. Joel's up there now working the area like it's a crime scene."

Abby swallowed hard. "It was just one shot. Maybe it was an accident?"

Cal lifted a brow. "I don't think so."

He helped his sister into a sitting position against the wall of the barn. "Come on, let's get comfortable. We're not going anywhere until we get the all clear."

An hour later after two more contractions by Fiona,

a good bit of whining from Tiffany and some under-the-breath muttering from Cal, he finally got the call he was waiting for.

Abby had just breathed a sigh of relief because once Fiona got still, her contractions stopped.

Cal opened the door to the barn and Abby looked around him. She saw an SUV headed toward them, chugging through the snow, the chains caked with the powdery stuff. But at least it was coming.

Two men she recognized as Joel and Mitchell got out of the vehicle, facing the trees where the shot had come from. They both had on bulletproof vests. "Y'all can come on out," Joel hollered. "We followed his tracks to the edge of the road. Looked like he used some kind of snowmobile to get away fast. But I'm pretty sure he's gone. Tracks coming in and going out."

Cal shook his head. "He came prepared, then."

"Yep. Zane insisted on continuing the search, but we don't think he'll find anything new."

They walked into the house where Cal and Jesse helped Fiona to the couch. Tiffany went to the toy box in the corner that was kept especially for her.

Cal looked up from his phone, his expression grim. "Asheville's covered up with snow and ice. Most likely we'd be able to make it with the chains on the tires." He looked at Fiona. "However, I don't want to take a chance on being stranded on the side of the road with you having contractions. Might be best if you just stay here."

"No!" Abby burst out.

Cal looked at her, compassion in his eyes. "Let's see what happens over the next several hours."

Abby felt the heat rise into her face and wanted to tell him by then it might be too late. Fiona breathed a sigh and lay back on the pillows, her hands cupped in a protective gesture under her belly.

Abby watched the second hand tick around, counting off the minutes. Once, twice, three times. Four. Five. "Anymore contractions?" Although she felt sure she would notice if one hit Fiona, she asked anyway.

Fiona shook her head, but Abby wasn't ready to breathe another sigh of relief yet.

Fiona sat up. "Someone needs to take me to my husband. Now. I'm not having this baby without him."

Abby laid a hand on the woman's arm. As much as she didn't want to do it, she had to convince the woman to stay. She hated it, but Cal was right. "You simply can't take the chance. You've had several contractions that finally stopped. You need to stay in bed for the rest of the day and probably tomorrow, too. I'm afraid if you start out of here, not knowing how the roads are, you might just have that baby in the back of the car."

Fiona simply stared at Abby. "Why do you know so much about medicine?" Recognition finally lit her eyes. "You knew exactly what to do with Joseph, you sound knowledgeable about how to tell when a baby's coming. Why?"

Fiona had been so distraught, Abby wondered if she'd even noticed what was going on in the barn. Apparently so.

"I've had a lot of training."

"She's a doctor," Cal said.

"A doctor!" Cal's mother let out a surprised laugh. "Well, how about that?"

"Yep." Cal's eyes were as warm as his eyes when he said, "She saved Holly and Eli's little Daniel. Apparently, he was choking and turning blue when Abby took over and saved his life."

"Well, I'll be…" Mrs. McIvers stared at Abby in wonder and Abby shifted, uncomfortable with the praise. After all, if she hadn't stayed, none of this would have happened. Except maybe Daniel wouldn't still be alive. Maybe God had used her after all.

Glancing around the sweet people who'd taken her in without question, nursed her back to health and protected against the person after her, Abby knew she needed to come clean.

"I think I know who the person who shot at Joseph might be."

TWELVE

Now that she had all eyes on her for a different reason, she wished she'd kept her mouth shut. But she hadn't and they were waiting for an answer.

Before she could say anything, Jesse stomped into the house. "All right, Ms. Justine. I got the car ready for you, but it's snowing again. If you're going to the hospital, we gotta git."

Justine crossed the room to take her daughter's hands in hers. "I'll be there for him, honey. Joseph would understand and want what's best for you and the baby. Please don't be stubborn about this. As soon as his parents get there, I'll head home and try to bring Dylan with me to deliver the baby if that's what we need to do. All right?"

Fiona's eyes went wide. "Have the baby here? I know I said I might like to, but after those last two contractions, I'm officially joining the 'I'm a wimp club.' I think I want an epidural and every other kind of pain medication they'll give me. I don't think doing the natural childbirth thing is for me. I'm coming with you."

She stood.

And a pained expression twisted her features. Grasping her belly, she froze, waited for the contraction to pass.

Then slowly lowered herself back to the couch. Tears filled her eyes. "You're right. I can't take the chance," she whispered.

Abby looked at her watch ready to time the contractions once again.

Fiona looked at her mother. "What if you get stuck?"

"Well, at least I won't have to worry about having a baby if I do." Abby could see the woman's angst. Go be with the seriously hurt son-in-law who may be dying or stay with the daughter who may have her first grandchild while she was gone.

Turmoil churned inside Abby. If she'd only left and kept going instead of allowing her heart to be swayed by Cal's sweet words and comforting presence.

Mrs. McIvers studied the little girl playing in the den. "What do I do about Tiffany?" she wondered out loud.

"You can leave her here with us," Abby found herself saying. "Zane will be down soon and if we need him to, he can take care of her." Meaning if Fiona ended up having the baby, Abby wouldn't have to juggle delivering Fiona's child and watching Tiffany.

Soon, Justine was hugging Fiona goodbye and Jesse led her out the door leaving Cal and Abby to hover over Fiona.

Abby took another look at her watch.

Seven minutes since the last contraction.

She walked into the kitchen and poured a glass of water. Back in the den, she handed the drink to Fiona. "Here, drink this. You don't want to get dehydrated."

Curiosity overshadowed the intense worry in Fiona's eyes. "Thank you." The woman took a few sips, then asked, "Why didn't you tell us you were a doctor? Why did you lie about your name?"

Abby flushed and sighed. "Because that's what one

does when one tries to run from the past. Unfortunately, I haven't turned out to be very good at it." A lump formed in her throat. "Which is why I believe Joseph is now hurt. I owe you all a huge apology," she whispered.

Cal reached out and squeezed her fingers. "Will you tell us everything so we can help?"

Everything? She wasn't quite sure about that. A glance toward Tiffany showed the little girl still engrossed in entertaining herself with a video game. "My sister, Keira, died." She stopped, not wanting Fiona to know that Keira had died giving birth. Some things were better left unspoken. Cal knew that part of the story and he knew why she paused. He shot her a grateful look as Abby picked up with, "She died about three months ago. Long story short, my family blames me because I'm a doctor and couldn't save her. Most of all, my brother-in-law, Reese, blames me. He threatened to... um...make me suffer the rest of my life." Abby swallowed the tears that threatened to erupt. "That was him in the bus station the day I collapsed." She frowned. "At least I think it was. I honestly don't know if I was hallucinating or if I really saw him."

As she recounted the story, Abby kept an eye on Fiona. Still no more contractions. A sense of relief flowed through her. Maybe the contractions would simply stop. So she silently prayed. And surprised herself by doing so.

But she realized God was drawing her back to Him. Showing her how much she needed Him.

Abby took a deep breath, Cal's fingers still wrapped around hers giving her courage. "I never would have believed he could say something like that. He's always been a gentle soul, but when Keira died, something inside him…changed. Hardened." Died with her sister, she wanted to say. Instead, she shook her head. "I don't want to believe it's him." Agony filled her. "But what else can I believe? He started showing up at my work, he would sit in his car and stare at me as I went into the grocery store and would be waiting when I came out. And after the restraining order went into effect, it got worse, believe it or not. I only saw Reese one time after the restraining order and that was the day before I decided to leave. I think he was trying to approach me, but one of my partners was with me and Reese didn't attempt to come near me." Abby's voice trembled. "I finally couldn't stand it any longer, so I ran."

Cal's jaw firmed. "Did you report him to the police?"

"Yes."

"And?"

"They said there was nothing they could do."

Cal gave a disgusted snort. "Sure, there is."

Not when it's one of their own, she wanted to say. "I truly thought the restraining order would help, but it didn't. Not really." Abby remembered the judge Reese had complained about. The one he'd said was as corrupt as the day was long, but he just couldn't prove it. It was the judge's son Reese had arrested for drunk driving and wouldn't make the charges go away when the judge had a fit.

The man had been happy to give her the restraining order against Reese Kirkpatrick. Abby felt about as low as a snake resorting to using an alleged corrupt judge, but she'd been at her wit's end.

"Did he violate the order?" Cal asked.

"No." And he hadn't. But he hadn't had to. His fellow cop buddies had picked up where Reese had left off and delivered his message loud and clear. They'd stopped her for every little traffic infraction, never writing her a ticket, but inconveniencing her enough that she became afraid to drive.

Cal frowned as his phone rang. "Excuse me. It's Eli."

He walked into the kitchen and Abby turned to Fiona. "I'm sorry."

"Abby, you don't need to apologize."

Abby smiled her sadness. "Thanks." She changed the subject. "How are the contractions?"

"Stopped, I think."

"That's good. The baby would be fine if he or she decided to come now, but maybe he'll wait until after the snow stops."

Fiona grimaced. "I have a feeling I should have gone with Mom and Jesse regardless of the contractions."

Abby had that same feeling, but didn't have time to dwell on it.

"I'm hungry," Tiffany suddenly said. "Can I have a snack?"

Abby stood. "Sure, come on in the kitchen and I'll slice you an apple."

Once Abby had the fruit cut up for Tiffany, the little girl asked, "Can I watch a movie?"

At a loss for an answer, Abby looked at Fiona. Fiona nodded. "In the spare bedroom, there's a television set up for her. She knows what to do."

Tiffany skipped down the hall toward the room with her bowl of fruit clutched in both hands. Soon Abby could hear the video playing and Tiffany singing along.

Cal came back into the room, his frosty eyes on Abby. "Eli did a little checking. You left out a few details in your story, didn't you?"

Abby's heart dropped like a stone to the bottom of the lake. So, he now knew.

Cal stepped farther into the room. "You didn't tell me that your brother-in-law was *Detective* Reese Kirkpatrick."

Cal couldn't believe he'd been so stupid. He'd known all along she'd been hiding something, but this blew him away. "You're running from the cops?"

"No." Her voice was even, no hint of emotion behind it. "Not *the* cops. *A* cop. One—" she held up her right index finger "—cop."

Cal stared at her, his mind processing the information Eli had just given him. Her record was practically squeaky clean. No hint of any kind of illegal activity. Just one parking ticket.

As much as he hated to admit it, Cal knew it was possible her brother-in-law wasn't on the up and up. His own sheriff had been arrested almost three years ago and now sat in a jail cell in Asheville. His good friend and fellow cop, Mark Sawls, had killed his own wife in a domestic violence episode.

But for the most part, Cal knew the majority of cops were honest, hardworking men and women doing the mostly thankless job because that was what they wanted to do, felt called to do.

And yet here was another cop being blamed for unethical, possibly illegal actions. It made him sick.

But was it true?

Abby had withheld a lot of information from them. She'd lied about her name, her background, who she was running from.

Then again, he could tell she was honestly scared of her brother-in-law.

Because a cop was after her and she knew she didn't have a chance against him? It wasn't a far-fetched idea.

The room echoed the silence surrounding him. Fiona clutched her cell phone, desperate for word from their mother about Joseph and looking stunned at the bombshell Cal had just dropped on her.

He knew what she was thinking. He knew if he could see into his sister's mind, he'd see her picturing Brianne. And he was thinking about Mark.

Taking a deep breath, he knew he had to give Abby the benefit of the doubt. If he didn't and he was wrong, she could wind up dead, too. And he couldn't live with another woman's death on his hands.

Abby sat, head ducked, hair swinging around her pale face. His heart went out to her and yet he felt angry at her reticence to confide in him.

She finally lifted her head. "Yes, he's a detective. But more than that, he's a very angry, bitter man who lost his wife." She still didn't mention the baby. "Now he has revenge on his mind and I'm the one he's focusing on."

The defeat in her voice stirred his compassion. And yet... "You really believe he wants to hurt you this bad?"

Abby paused and he could see the doubt flickering in her eyes. "I don't want to think so."

"But you do."

"Yes."

Before she could say any more, Fiona let out a low groan. The pain in his sister's face nearly made him panic. He looked at Abby. "Is she going to have this baby now?"

Abby shot him a sour look. "Not if the contractions stop."

"So make them stop."

The look Abby and Fiona exchanged said his male input wasn't needed—or wanted.

Tiffany came from the back bedroom. "Where's my grandpa?"

Grateful for the distraction, Cal reached for the little girl and picked her up. Keeping one eye on Fiona's clenched jaw, he said, "He's out doing me a favor. Are you tired of your video?"

"Nope, I'm going to go finish it."

Cal set her down and she went back to the room. He looked back at his sister.

When the contraction eased, Fiona leaned her head back and Abby looked at her watch. "How much time between that one and the last one?"

"Eight minutes."

"So when do we start getting worried?"

Abby smiled, but Cal thought it looked a bit forced. "Not right now." She patted Fiona's hand. "You're doing fine. We'll time them and see what happens. You just lie here and relax."

Fiona rolled her eyes and looked annoyed—and scared. "How am I supposed to relax? I'm so worried about Joseph and Mom and Jesse…" she whispered.

The phone buzzed in her hand and Fiona lifted it to her ear. "Hello?"

Cal wanted to tell her to put it on speaker phone, but she was listening so intently that he didn't want to interrupt.

When she hung up, she bit her lip and looked at Cal. "That was Mom. She said the roads are bad."

He tensed. "Are they okay?"

"So far. They're having to go really slow and they got stuck once. Jesse managed to get them out so they're moving again. She said it was a good thing I didn't go with them." She sniffed. "And she told me not to have this baby until she gets back." A puff of laughter escaped her and Cal smiled. That sounded like his mother.

Abby rose. "I think I'd better stay close by, Fiona. Do you mind if I just sleep up here near you? In case you need something?"

"I can do that," Cal said.

"No." Fiona shook her head before Abby could respond. "You need to keep watch on the ranch and make sure that person after Abby doesn't come back. You can stay here, but I want Abby up here, too."

Cal thought about it and nodded. "It might not be a bad idea to keep you two together just in case."

Abby gulped. "Just in case?"

He shrugged, not wanting to frighten them any more than they already were, but if someone, like Detective Reese Kirkpatrick, was determined to get at them, he wanted them watching their backs and keeping the doors locked. "Just a precaution."

His phone rang again. "Hello?"

"Eli again."

"What's up?"

"I found something interesting about Ms. O'Sullivan's brother-in-law."

Cal felt his gut clench in spite of himself. "What's that?"

"He's got a spotless record. In fact, he's been the recipient of just about every cop award out there."

"But?" Cal waited knowing something was coming.

"I talked to his captain. After Reese's wife died, he didn't want to take any time off. Said he couldn't sit at home and stare at four walls and not go completely over the edge."

"I can understand that." If something like that happened to him, he'd feel the same way.

"Yeah, but his captain told him he didn't have a choice."

Cal winced. "Ouch."

"Anyway, Detective Kirkpatrick took his two weeks, but came into the office every day at some point until he was chased off. Said he was spending his vacation at the office and if his captain didn't like it, he could fire him."

Also sounded like something Cal would do. So far, he was having a hard time picturing the man as a bad cop. "Then what?"

"He wouldn't take time off to grieve for his dead family, but took a leave of absence two days after Abby left town."

A bad feeling crawled into his stomach to stay. "And?"

"And no one's heard from him since. His parents are both dead. He was raised in foster homes for the most part. No one wanted to adopt him because he was such a troublemaker. But apparently around his junior or senior year, the school resource officer at his high school took an interest in him."

"Did you talk to this guy?"

"Sure did. His name's Glenn Pierce. And he's adamant that Reese would never do what he's being accused of, that he's a good man who's lived through a world of hurt."

Cal sighed. "Man, I don't know what to think."

"I know." Eli sounded dubious. Then he said, "His in-laws, Abby's parents, say they haven't talked to him since their daughter Keira's funeral and they have no idea where he'd go." A pause. "However, I did talk to

Detective Kirkpatrick's partner. The man said that Reese was messed up pretty bad. Not sleeping, not eating. Said his wife's and baby's deaths have just about destroyed him."

"Enough that he would seek revenge against the woman he considered responsible for their deaths?"

"Maybe." He paused and Cal heard papers shuffling in the background. "Kirkpatrick must have scared her pretty bad. She managed to get a restraining order approved."

"Yeah, she told me. But if he left two days after Abby, I don't see how it's possible that Abby may have seen him in the bus station the day she arrived in town."

"I don't think she could have even though it looks like he was right behind her on the same route that she took. He didn't even try to hide the fact that he was following her. But the dates don't match up. I don't think Abby could have seen him in the bus station."

Frowning, Cal considered that. "We'll just have to ask him when we catch up to him. Can you get his picture out to everyone? All of the hotels and bed and breakfasts, too?"

"Already done."

Cal rubbed his eyes. "All right. How's the weather looking? I haven't had a chance to keep up with it in the past few hours."

"Looking pretty grim."

"Great. Look, my mother and Jesse are headed for the hospital in Asheville. Fiona's having contractions. Can you have the ambulance on call in case we need it?" The town of Rose Mountain had only one.

Cal winced at Eli's short, humorless laugh. "Cal, that ambulance isn't going anywhere anytime soon. The roads are already covered up. Later this evening, they're just going to be ice. You'll need a tank to get off your place at that point."

"Or the snowmobile." Cal wondered how it would work getting Fiona on the machine and to the hospital. He didn't see that happening. The bad feeling in his gut didn't go away.

"Or that."

"Thanks, Eli. Keep me posted on anything else you come up with."

"Will do."

Cal hung up the phone, his thoughts racing. He walked back into the den to find Fiona in a restless sleep, her forehead pinched and mouth drawn, and Abby pacing.

She looked up as he walked in and Cal blanched at the tears swimming in her eyes. "I'm sorry," she whispered. "I'm so sorry."

He couldn't stand it. Reaching out, he pulled her into his arms and marveled at how well she fit next to him. "It'll be all right, Abby. It's really not your fault."

She shuddered and wrapped her arms around his waist. "I feel like it is. I feel like everything's my fault lately and I'm at a loss about what to do with it."

"Let God handle it."

"God let Keira and baby Emma die. I don't want to trust Him with anything else." She shuddered.

Cal closed his eyes wondering how to convince her that God still had her in the palm of His hand and knew what was best even when that best seemed the worst she could ever imagine. "Do you believe God is who He says He is?"

"I don't know. I want to. I used to."

"He's the one true God. He died for you because He loved you so much. And that you have to believe that and accept that to be with Him when you die? Do you believe that?"

"Yes," she whispered, "I do believe that."

"Then you've got to believe everything else He says because you can't pick and choose which parts of the Bible are true and which ones you just don't like."

"Like all things work together for the good of those who believe in Him?" She bit her lip and the tears clouding her eyes dripped.

"Yep." He swiped one from her cheek and felt its warmth against his finger. It broke his heart.

"But what good will come of Keira's death?" she cried into his chest. "I can't see it."

He hugged her tighter. "You can't see it now, but maybe one day, He'll make it all clear for you."

"I feel like He let me down," she mumbled her words, still muffled against him. "Not only am I angry with Him, I'm…disappointed in Him."

Cal nodded and kissed her head. "I know."

Low, quiet sobs shook her and, helpless, he simply held her until she had no more tears left to cry.

Abby had to admit that while she felt like a complete idiot after her little breakdown in Cal's arms, she also felt better. Fortunately, Fiona slept through it and Cal didn't seem to be terribly put out that Abby had used his shirt to mop her tears.

He'd finally placed a gentle kiss on her forehead, then showed her to the spare bedroom giving her time and space to compose herself. He told her he was going to join Zane in a ride around the property as he didn't want the man going off by himself.

"Keep the doors locked and stay away from the windows. I've got my cell phone. Call me if you need anything."

Now, all alone, she pulled her own cell phone from her pants pocket and dialed her work number.

"Hello?"

"Hello, Lisa, it's Abby."

A gasp met her statement. "Abby? How are you? *Where* are you?"

"I left you a note. I took a little vacation."

"That note didn't explain anything, but—" she paused "—I guess we all understand why you need a little time off."

Abby winced. "Yeah." She wasn't in the mood for small talk. "I need to speak with Dr. Owens. Is he there?" One never called Dr. Samuel Owens by his given name. It didn't matter if one was a colleague or a receptionist or the mayor. He was Dr. Owens.

Lisa sighed. "No, he's not here. His wife had her baby last night."

Oh, right. She'd forgotten the man was a soon-to-be father. "Did he deliver the baby?" she asked.

"Yes." The smile in Lisa's voice said everything had gone well.

"Okay, what about Randall?"

"No." Lisa drew the word out into two syllables. "He's not here, either. But Dr. Wert and Dr. Ishmael are here."

Abby considered them and sighed. "No, I really need to speak with Randall." Randall had been there during the dark days after her sister's death. He'd often come by the office when she'd stayed late, encouraging her to go home and rest. And walking her to her car when she needed him, too. "Where is he?"

"His mother took a turn for the worse. He left about

a week ago. He checks in every day, though. Do you want me to tell him to call you?"

"No, that's all right. I've got his cell phone number."

"Sure. Anything else I can do for you?"

Abby thought about it. "No, I guess not. Thanks, Lisa. Hopefully, I'll see you soon. If not, have a merry Christmas."

"You, too."

Abby hung up, no longer worried about Reese tracking her through her cell phone. Somehow, he'd managed to follow her in spite of all of her precautions.

Now she just had to figure out how to keep him from unleashing his bitterness on the family she'd come to care about.

Cal sat on top of the horse and stared down at the house where Abby and Fiona were. He felt a little uneasy at the thought of leaving them alone, but he wasn't riding far and could see the house from where he was. He had his cell phone and they had his number.

However, Zane had ridden farther in the direction the bullet had come from.

A copse of trees had made the perfect cover for the shooter. A direct view of the barn and the house—and everything in between. The man had been a good shot. The distance was about half a mile. If the horse hadn't spooked at the cat, Joseph might very well have a bullet inside of him.

The fact that he'd had a horse fall on him might actually be a blessing in disguise. If he'd been shot, he might have died instantly.

Then again, he might be dying slowly at this very moment. Cal refused to believe that. *Please, God, let him live to see his child. My sister needs him. His baby needs a father.*

Cal sighed and waited for Zane to come back over the hill. The wind whipped around him and Cal was grateful for the warm hat that sat snug on his head, covering his ears. Sheepskin gloves kept his hands from freezing, but the jeans he had on weren't quite warm enough.

But he didn't plan to be out here much longer.

Movement caught his eye and his hand went to his rifle. A second later, Zane appeared, rifle in one hand and something in the other.

"What you got?" Cal asked.

Zane rode closer. "Found a casing." He handed it over to Cal who studied it. "A Winchester 40 S & W." Cal grunted as he shifted his own Winchester. "Well, he's got good taste in weapons."

"Surprised he didn't take it with him." Zane rubbed his jaw and Cal watched the man scan the hills, his eyes alert, sharp and ready for anything.

"Might have heard the chopper, thought it was the cops and decided it was time to get out while he could." Cal tried to picture the events in his mind and it was the only thing that made sense.

"Possibly."

"I'm also curious why he shot only one time," Cal muttered, pocketing the casing. He'd turn it over to Eli to match it up with the bullet found in the yard. And if a weapon was found that could possibly be the one used by the shooter, the casing would be matched with the weapon. Cal looked down at the house. All looked quiet. "He had to have seen that he didn't hit anything. I don't understand why he didn't try again."

Zane shrugged. "Maybe something scared him off?"

"Maybe," Cal agreed. "See anything else?"

"Nope. I rode along the fence line for a while, the area closest to the house, and didn't see any new tracks."

Cal allowed his shoulders to relax a fraction. "All right, let's get out of this weather and check up on Joseph."

Zane nodded and turned his horse toward the barn.

Cal looked down at Fiona's house once more and thought how peaceful it looked right now.

Unfortunately, he knew that looks could be deceiving.

THIRTEEN

Abby sat in the recliner and stared at the television mounted on the wall. The weather channel ran nonstop news about the snow/ice storm pelting the southeast. And she was right in the middle of it.

With a pregnant woman and a five-year-old.

Ten minutes ago she'd checked on Tiffany. The little girl had fallen asleep in front of the television and Abby had covered her with a light blanket.

Now her mind circled back to Fiona. She wasn't sure at what point she'd realized she was probably going to have to help deliver Fiona's baby, but the thought was now at the forefront of her mind. There was no way Fiona could safely be transported off the ranch to a hospital.

Which meant a home birth.

The thought made her hands shake and her stomach swirl. She couldn't do it.

But she might have to.

God, please...

The prayer slipped through her mind easily, naturally. She'd missed Him. With a dawning knowledge, she realized she wasn't mad at God anymore, just very, very sad that He'd allowed her sister to die.

Abby strode to the attached bathroom to splash water on her face and pull in a deep breath. A look in the mirror didn't help matters. She found herself staring straight into terror-filled eyes.

What was she going to do? She couldn't leave now because of the weather. And she wouldn't leave Fiona alone anyway. Not at this point in her pregnancy.

"Abby?"

"Coming."

Abby opened the door to find Fiona standing at the end of the hallway. "Are you all right?"

Fiona looked tired, wan, worried, but she nodded even as tears filled her eyes. "I'll be all right. I just got a call from the hospital. You were right. Joseph had a lot of internal bleeding. He's in surgery."

"But he made it there safely." And he made it alive. "What about your mother and Jesse?"

"They're still fighting the weather, but are making progress. Mom said she expects they'll get there in shortly. It's stopped snowing for now."

"Really?" She hadn't noticed. Together they walked into the den. "Maybe that'll make it a little easier for them." Abby motioned to Fiona's stomach. "Any more contractions?"

"No."

"Good."

Fiona gave a wan smile. "Yeah."

A shadow passed outside the den window and Abby felt her neck muscles tense. A low hum reached her ears. There were no blinds or shades to draw and she felt exposed. Of course out here in the middle of three-thousand acres, Fiona and Joseph wouldn't feel the need to cover their windows. However, Abby couldn't help wishing for a little bit of cover right now.

Without alarming Fiona, Abby moved toward the window, staying close to the side, doing her best not to be too obvious.

The wide-open fields beyond the house would make it hard for someone to sneak up. But the trees planted strategically around the house would make it easy for someone to hide if they somehow managed to slink across the openness.

Looking out, she saw nothing to alarm her and she no longer heard anything. It was probably just the sun moving, a tree swaying, anything but that there was someone outside.

And yet, she wasn't going to discount the possibility. Not after her past few weeks. And what had been that sound? She couldn't put her finger on it, but her internal alarm was screeching. "It looks beautiful out there. A winter landscape waiting to be painted." She kept her voice even, her tone conversational even as her eyes scanned the landscape.

"Brianne would have done it justice."

Abby glanced over her shoulder. "Tell me about her?"

A sad smile crossed Fiona's lips. "She was my cousin. And a friend. My best friend. She was also a victim of domestic violence."

"Cal told me a little about her."

"Her husband, a cop, murdered her." Fiona's lips twisted and her forehead pulled down into a frown. Tears formed and she blinked them back. "That's one of the reasons why—" She broke off and bit her lip. Abby gave her time to find the words she seemed to be looking for. "When you said you were running from someone we were so intent on protecting you. We just felt like we should have done more for Brianne, but because Mark was a cop..."

"And it's hard to believe a cop would do such a thing." Abby heard the derision in her voice and couldn't help it.

But Fiona didn't seem offended by it. Instead, she nodded. "Yes." Her jaw stiffened. "He was an excellent actor. Played the part of the wounded husband very well. Couldn't understand why Brianne would do the things she was doing to him." Fiona shook her head. "Brianne finally quit saying anything."

"Did you believe her?"

"Yes, but I was the only one. Even Cal wasn't sure what to believe."

"I'm sorry." Abby felt sick for the poor woman and the family who couldn't protect her.

"It's done. But—" she pulled in a deep breath and looked at Abby "—we can help others. Like you."

"Do you think Cal believes me?"

"I think he's willing to give you the benefit of the doubt. Your brother-in-law being a cop won't stop Cal from doing his best to find the truth."

"I told you the truth." Abby kept her voice neutral.

Fiona looked at her and smiled a soft smile. "And I believe you. And I think Cal does, too. But he'll have to have indisputable evidence."

"Because Reese is a cop."

"Partly."

Abby felt the chill deep inside her. Reese would know how to cover his tracks and he would do it with the utmost care. He also loved the outdoors. Hunting, fishing, camping. He would know how to survive out here in the cold and snow.

Then again, a lot of people she knew had the same skills. Did it necessarily have to be Reese? They sat there in silence for the next thirty minutes, watching the weather channel, lost in their own thoughts.

Then Abby said, "I can't figure it out."

"What?" Fiona, settled onto the couch, had the remote control in her left hand.

"Reese had a number of chances to get to me before I ran like a scared rabbit. But he didn't. He intimidated me, yes. He threatened to make me suffer the rest of my life. True. But he never actually acted violent."

Fiona grimaced. "It doesn't take much to go from stalking and watching to killing."

Abby gave a slow nod and went back to her vigil at the window. Careful to stay to the side, she glanced out. Still nothing.

She had just about convinced herself the shadow had been the sun. And then Cal rode into view looking small and far away, but she could tell it was him. "You don't use vehicles much on this ranch, do you?"

Fiona laughed, the first real smile she'd offered since Joseph's accident. "Actually, yes, we do. A lot. But in this kind of weather, it makes more sense to use the horses—or the snowmobiles."

Abby felt a flush creep up her neck. "Well, that was a stupid question, wasn't it?"

"No, not at all."

"You're sweet."

A knock sounded on the door and Abby walked to peek through the window.

Cal and Zane.

She unlocked and opened the door to let the men in. They'd tied their horses just outside instead of putting them in the barn. Which meant they planned to use them again.

For what?

Cal stomped the snow from his boots and hung his hat on the hook behind the door. Zane followed suit and asked, "Where's Tiffany?"

"She fell asleep watching the video."

Zane shook his head. "Her mama doesn't let her watch them that much, so she takes full advantage when she gets to come over to the McIverses'." The smile in his eyes said he didn't mind.

Fiona looked up from her spot on the couch. "Did you see anything suspicious?"

Cal shook his head. "Maybe some more tracks. I got the snowmobile out."

"Mom just called me five minutes ago and said they'd made it to the hospital. Joseph is the same, still in surgery. She said she'd call as soon as she knew anything else."

Abby stood silent, watching and listening.

Zane walked into the kitchen and Cal turned his attention to Abby. "How are you feeling?"

"Stupid," she muttered.

And then he smiled. A slow, lingering, soft smile that made her heart flip and her stomach swoop.

And her mind go, "uh-oh."

She was falling in love with him. Hard and fast and irrevocably. In love.

Her knees shook at the realization and Abby felt her palms start to sweat.

She wanted to run away. As far as she could flee.

But she couldn't.

She was stuck.

Snowbound with a man who made her pulse do crazy things.

A throat clearing made them both jump. Zane stood

in the doorway of the kitchen with a knowing look on his face.

Abby saw Cal's cheeks flush and knew she had a matching color in her own face.

Zane said, "I'm going to head on over to the bunk house. Most everyone's gone to be with family for the holidays. If it's all right to leave Tiffany here, I reckon I'll hang around and keep an eye on things down there."

Cal nodded. "We'd appreciate it. Until we catch this guy, I might need your eyes and ears. And it might be safer for Tiffany to be up here in the house."

Zane frowned, worry reflected in his eyes. He hesitated. "Maybe I ought to take her with me."

"Whatever you want to do," Cal said.

Indecision flickered, then Zane said, "Reckon you're right. She's probably better off here."

He left and Abby glanced at Fiona who'd stood and begun to pace, the phone clutched in her hand. Abby understood the woman's restlessness but wished she'd sit down. Unless... "Fiona, are you having any more contractions?"

"No, I just can't sit still." She resumed her trek back and forth across the room.

Cal frowned at his sister but simply said, "Zane doesn't have any family around here other than Tiffany right now. He usually joins us for Christmas."

Abby felt a pang. What would she do for Christmas? The snow on the ground said she might be joining the McIvers family, too. The speculation in Cal's eyes said he was thinking the same thing.

Abby fingered the phone in her pocket. Should she try her parents' number? It had been a little over two months since she'd tried. After the last time, she'd decided they would call her when they were ready.

And nothing. They were hurt and grieving.

Well, so was she and she needed them. They needed each other.

Making up her mind, she said, "Excuse me a minute, please. I need to make a phone call."

Back in her room, she dialed the number she didn't have to look up. After four rings, she was just about to hang up when her father's voice came on the line. "Hello?"

Abby's throat threatened to close up on her. "Hi, Dad. Are you speaking to me yet?"

Silence.

But she was encouraged. She knew he had caller ID and he'd answered the phone anyway. And he hadn't hung up when he heard her voice.

"Dad?"

"I'm here." His low husky bass voice brought back lots of good memories. And recent bad ones. Her heart filled with grief and the desperate desire for reconciliation.

"I'm sorry, Dad. I don't know what else to say. I need you and mom to forgive me." She closed her eyes and drew in a deep breath. "I need you to still love me," she whispered.

Abby heard his breath catch and wondered what he was thinking. She wished she could see his face.

"Gabby girl…"

Her heart thudded. The fact that he would use his childhood nickname for her gave her hope. But how long would he stay on the line? She got control of her emotions and cleared her throat. "Before you hang up, I need to ask you something."

"What's that?"

"Have you heard from Reese lately?"

"No." He sounded puzzled. "Why?"

"Because someone's been trying to hurt me and he's the only person I can think of who has a motive." Abby didn't bother to mince her words or pull punches.

"What?" he nearly yelled. Well, at least she had his attention.

"I'm okay," she hurried to reassure him. "I've got some good friends who are helping me out, but if you see Reese, please try to talk some sense into him. For his sake, if not for me."

"Abby, I…I don't know what to say. What do you want me to do? I mean…"

"Just say you'll talk to him."

"Yes, of course. I promise. If I see him."

"Thanks, Dad." She didn't want the conversation to end. It was the first one they'd had without him casting blame. Or weeping uncontrollably.

"I love you, Dad."

More silence, then she thought she heard, "Love you, too, Gabby girl," before the quiet click of the phone disconnecting echoed across the line.

FOURTEEN

After all of the excitement over the past two weeks, Cal couldn't believe how quiet the past two days had been. Joseph had come through surgery and was recovering nicely. Joseph's parents had managed to drive down from Raleigh. What should have been a four-hour trip turned into a twelve-hour nightmare, but they'd made it.

Fiona hadn't had any more contractions and Zane had declared the ranch intruder-free.

At least for now.

And Abby.

Abby had waited on Fiona hand and foot, her watchful eye taking in every detail of Fiona's health. She'd also seemed to enjoy taking care of little Tiffany when Zane worked the ranch.

His heart expanded with emotions he wasn't quite ready to deal with but not so sure he wanted to ignore either.

Cal wasn't so dense to not realize what was going on with him and his heart. He'd fallen hard for the quiet, troubled doctor and he wasn't ready to tell her goodbye yet. However, her accusations against her brother-in-law made his gut clench.

Was he dealing with another cop like Brianne's husband? A man who could lie and charm his way out of just about any situation imaginable?

He hoped not.

Cal walked up the steps of Fiona's apartment where he'd made himself at home in case his sister or Abby needed him. Abby had moved upstairs like she'd offered.

But in spite of the quiet, Cal wasn't ready to leave them alone or trust that the man had given up on Abby. If anything, the quiet simply tightened his tension as he waited for the next move.

At the top of the stairs, he found Abby in the kitchen pouring a cup of coffee. When she saw him, she handed him the first cup, then filled another for herself.

"Thanks," he said, then asked, "how's she doing?"

"Okay for now. No contractions and she's relieved that Joseph is doing all right. She just wishes she could be with him." Sorrow flickered across her eyes and he knew she was once again blaming herself for Joseph's situation.

"Of course she does. But it's not possible and it's not your fault." When she looked like she might argue, he gestured to the open laptop on the kitchen table. "What are you working on?"

Abby sighed and her shoulders slumped, defeat written in every line of her body. Concerned, he placed a hand on her arm. "Hey, what's going on?"

She looked up and studied him. A shudder rippled through her even as she seemed to make up her mind about something. "I need help," she whispered. "I can't do this on my own anymore."

"Abby, you don't have to. Talk to me."

She nodded. "Okay. Come here."

Curious, he followed her to the table. She sat in the chair and jiggled the wireless mouse. Cal looked over her shoulder and couldn't help noticing the fresh scent of her newly washed hair mingling with the smells of the coffee and toast.

He liked it.

He was glad she was here this morning. He really wanted to help her, to have her trust him. He wanted her to let him comfort her.

Looking up, she caught him watching and he didn't look away. Instead he leaned down to capture her lips with his.

He felt her freeze and wondered if she would pull back. But she didn't. Instead, she shifted to give him better access. His hand reached around to cup the back of her head. Lips still connected, she rose and wrapped her arms around his waist. Feelings and emotions long buried and forgotten about tumbled through him as his fingers wrapped themselves in the fiery strands of her hair.

His heart thudded against his chest as he reveled in their first kiss. And hoped it would be the first of many.

And then she pulled back, eyes wide and stunned, a red flush on her smooth cheeks.

He lifted a thumb to trace her cheekbone. "I'm not going to apologize for that."

Her eyes narrowed. "I'd hit you if you did."

Cal felt a grin tugging at the corners of his lips. An answering one echoed in her eyes.

He heard Fiona stirring in the other room and turned his attention back to the computer. "What did you want to show me?" He wondered if she could hear his struggle to breathe.

Taking his cue, she turned back to the computer and

pointed. "These are my patients' medical records. And please pretend I never showed you this stuff. I'm breaking a big rule by even discussing this with you, but I have to talk to someone or I'm going to go crazy." She looked back at him. "And I trust you."

Never had any four words sounded so good to his ears. Only three words would have sounded better, but he figured it was too soon for those.

Focusing, Cal listened as she explained about finding patients filed under her care. Patients she'd never seen before and then finding patients she *had* seen but had been billed for tests and procedures she'd never ordered.

"What does the total come to when you add up everything the various insurance companies have paid out?" he asked.

"Over half a million dollars."

Cal blinked. "That's some big bucks."

Abby nodded and stared at the screen. The flush on her cheeks had faded but not much. The sight made him smile and elation filled him. Not only did she trust him, she cared for him.

Instinct told him she didn't just go around kissing every guy she met. Which was fine with him. He was the same way. In fact, the last woman he'd kissed had been well over a year ago. She'd dumped him after six months together and moved to California.

Cal had been hurt at the time. Now he thanked God for it.

"It looks like it's me, Cal. Someone's set me up."

"Any ideas who?"

She chewed her lip and looked at him beneath lowered lashes. He narrowed his eyes and reached out to take her hand. "Who do you think it is?"

"Reese. It has to be."

Cal frowned. "And would he have access to this kind of information?"

"He's a detective. What would you do if you wanted to get into those files?"

"I'd have to get a court order."

She looked at him. "He's got friends in high places. What if this is what he meant by making me suffer the rest of my life? What if he's so mad about the fact that I let his wife die that he's out to discredit me, make sure I never practice medicine again? Or…make sure I spend a really long time in jail?"

Christmas Eve morning, Cal's mother wanted to come home and Cal was supposed to work part of the morning shift. Every deputy on the small force had agreed to put in a few hours so nobody would be stuck working the entire Christmas holidays. And they'd all agreed to stay on call in case of an emergency.

The snow had settled in at around a foot and a half. Temperatures hovered around freezing and Cal figured whoever was after Abby had holed up to wait out the weather.

But that didn't mean he was dropping his guard.

Zane promised to keep an eye on things while Cal ran into Asheville to pick up his mother who'd insisted Jesse stay in town with his family for Christmas.

Cal would take the snowmobile as far as town, work his five hours, then use the department's snow-ready SUV and head to Asheville.

Eli had okayed the use of the vehicle as long as Cal promised to do something that qualified as official business. Cal agreed. When his cell phone vibrated in his pocket, Cal cut the motor and pulled to a stop so he could hear.

"Hello?"

Eli said, "I just came across some mighty interesting information on Detective Kirkpatrick."

"What you got?"

"His car is parked in front of the hotel."

Cal jerked and nearly lost his balance on the snowmobile. "Come again?"

"I started running the plates on everyone at the hotel again. Last time we came up empty. This time, I came up with some interesting stuff, but the biggest one was your friend Reese."

"What room is he in?"

"Room 406, but he's not there. I sent Joel over to check and it's empty. The desk clerk said he left about two hours ago."

Frustration grabbed Cal. "Where'd he go?"

"To the car rental place. Guy said your man rented an SUV with chains on the tires."

Cold swirled inside Cal, a freezing chill that made the weather around him feel warm. "He's coming this way, isn't he? He's going after her."

"I'm not sure what to think, Cal. But it gets more interesting. He called me a bit ago with some crazy story about how he was investigating Abby and found some kind of insurance fraud. He said one of her partners is in town. Before he could say anything else, I lost the connection. The storm is messing with all cell reception. I also think he said something about heading to your place."

Cal's fear spiked.

"Why wait till now? Why not call yesterday or the day before?"

"I don't know, Cal, but you better get back there and find out."

"I'm on my way. I left them at home alone with Zane." Cal gritted his teeth and started planning what explanation he would give his mother about why he couldn't come get her.

"Zane's a good man," Eli said. "He can take care of things."

The chill deepened. "Not if he thinks things are fine. And I think things went from fine to bad the minute Detective Kirkpatrick rented that SUV. Sounds like we have a pretty determined man on our hands. I'll give Zane a call and tell him to be on the lookout until I get back home." A glint to the left caught his eye. "Keep me updated, Eli. Right now, I need to check something out." He hung up.

When Cal moved his head, he could see an object far in the distance. A car? He tensed. Still gripping his phone, he punched in Zane's number. No answer. When it went to voice mail, Cal said, "Zane, I think we're getting ready to have some unfriendly company. Keep your eyes open." Cal described the vehicle according to Eli and hung up. For good measure, he sent the man a text message telling him to check his voice mail.

The area between his shoulders itched. He started the snowmobile and took off to investigate what he'd seen. If someone was sitting up there with a rifle, it would be harder to hit a moving target.

Abby shivered as she stared out at the vast whiteness before her. No more snow fell, but clouds hovered overhead threatening more.

"Abby?"

Abby turned from the window to see Fiona standing

in the door. The woman's shocked expression sent her immediately to her side. "What is it? Are you all right?"

"Um…my water broke. I think. I mean, I'm pretty sure."

"But you have another week," Abby said dumbly.

Fiona let out a breathy laugh. "I don't think this little one really cares."

Abby shook her head and forced herself into professional mode. Of course the baby could come a week early. She had to get it together.

And not think about Keira.

"Okay," she said. "Then we've got some things to do."

"Like what?"

"Everything that entails getting you ready to have a baby."

As Abby gathered the necessary materials to prepare for a home birth, she watched Fiona pace.

No doubt Fiona was going to have this baby sometime today. Could be in a few hours. Could be in a few minutes.

Either way, she needed to let Cal know.

Grabbing her cell phone, she powered it up.

One missed call.

That could wait.

She dialed Cal's number and waited. It rang four times and went to voice mail. Frustrated, she left him a message to call her and that Fiona was in labor.

As Cal approached the area where he'd seen the object, he slowed.

A jeep?

And if there was a jeep, shouldn't there be a driver? Cal slid from the snowmobile and approached the vehicle, wariness making him edgy, his muscles tight and ready for action.

The driver's door caught his attention and his eyes honed in on the reddish handprint in the area of the handle. Blood.

He walked to the side and glanced in, trying to keep himself from being a target as best he could.

Empty.

His gaze landed back on the snow. Footprints led away from the car and drops of bright red glinted up at him.

"Who are you and what happened to you?" Cal whispered.

Wait a minute. He went to the back of the jeep. Harlan's rentals. Chains on the tires.

Had he come across Reese Kirkpatrick?

Relief surged through him. For some reason, the man was hurt. That would slow him down getting to Abby and Fiona. Cal shifted his weapon and pulled out his cell phone. He dialed Zane's number.

No answer.

Cal hung up and dialed Fiona's home number.

Abby answered on the third ring.

"Hello?"

She sounded out of breath.

"Are you all right?" he asked.

"Fiona's in labor."

His stomach dropped. "What?"

"Her water broke a little while ago."

"Why didn't you call?" he demanded.

"I did."

Her soft tone calmed him. A bit. "Sorry, I didn't mean to snap. I was on the snowmobile and didn't catch the phone's vibration, I guess. Is Zane there with you?"

"No, we haven't seen him. Why?"

"I found Reese's jeep. Keep an eye on the windows. Make sure all the doors are locked and call me if there's even a hint of a problem." A pause. "And here's Zane's number." He rattled off the digits. "I know Fiona has it somewhere, but I'm guessing she's probably not in the mood to find it."

"What are you doing?"

Cal hated to be the one to put the fear in her voice. "I'm going to find Reese before he gets to the house."

"I can't believe this," she whispered.

Her scared, soft voice made his gut clench. "Listen, your brother-in-law called Eli."

"He did what?" Fear tightened her words. "What did he say? Why would he call?"

"He said he'd been investigating you and found the insurance fraud stuff. He's on his way out here."

"Okay," she whispered and Cal wanted to reach through the line and hug her. "We'll be careful. Please stay in touch and let me know you're all right."

His heart filled at her worry. For him. "I will. And as soon as I find him, I'll call. If you see someone on the ranch who shouldn't be there, you call me immediately. Now you call Zane and fill him in, okay?"

"Sure."

He hung up the phone and called Eli back. After reporting his find to the sheriff who promised to send backup as soon as he could, Cal started following the footsteps that were quickly disappearing in the falling snow. He'd have to bring his A game. There was no guarantee backup would—or even could—arrive in time.

Abby held Fiona's hand as another contraction ripped through the woman. As the pain eased, Fiona breathed through pursed lips and relaxed. She looked at Abby, fear and excitement mingled in her gaze. "I'm having this baby soon, aren't I?"

"Looks like it." Abby smiled to cover her terror. She did her best to shove aside memories of another birth. Checking her cell phone, she noticed the battery going low. Great.

"What's wrong with Aunt Fiona?" Tiffany asked.

Abby turned to see the little girl standing in the doorway rubbing the sleep from her eyes. Abby stood and went to her. "She's getting ready to have a baby."

"Oh. Can I play with it?"

Abby heard Fiona smother a laugh.

"Soon, darling. But for now, we need you to help Aunt Fiona. Do you think you can do that?"

Tiffany cocked her head and yawned. "Maybe. What do I got to do?"

"Well…" Abby frantically thought. What could she do to occupy the little girl? "The baby's room is all ready, but I bet the bottles need washing. Would you want to do that?"

Tiffany's eyes went wide. "Sure. I help my mama all the time. I stand on a chair and make lots of bubbles and wash my baby doll's dishes."

"Perfect. Let's fill the sink up and you can get right to it. I know Fiona will appreciate it."

Abby looked at Fiona over Tiffany's head and Fiona nodded with a small smile on her lips. Then her lips flattened as another contraction hit her.

Abby took Tiffany by the hand and led her from the bedroom into the kitchen. She pulled a chair over and the little girl climbed up. Abby found the bottles in the cabinet already sterilized and ready for use.

She grabbed every last one of them and dumped them

in the sink. Once the sink was filled with warm water and "more and more bubbles," Tiffany got to work.

Abby left her and went down the hall to check on Fiona.

"I'm so glad you're here with me," Fiona said, tears standing in her eyes. "I wasn't worried about being pregnant and so far away from a hospital when I had Mom and Joseph out here with me. But my support system is gone and the weather isn't cooperating one bit."

"You'll be just fine," Abby soothed. And prayed it was true. Determination filled her even as worry consumed her. She had no way to monitor Fiona's blood pressure, her vitals, the baby's heartbeat.

A thought struck her. "Does your mother have a stethoscope?"

Fiona nodded. "Sure, she has her whole nursing bag up at her house."

Should she try to get it?

"How far is it to her house from here? About half a mile?" She just realized she'd never been in the main house.

"Yes, but—" Fiona's eyes went wide. "You're not going to leave me here alone, are you?" Panic bloomed on her face and Fiona shook her head. "What if the baby comes?"

"No, no, I'm not going anywhere." Not now anyway. "I'm thinking Zane could go for it." If he would answer his phone.

Fiona relaxed. "Don't scare me like that, please."

"Sorry."

"I'm going to try Zane again. I don't understand why he's not answering." But her stomach churned and she couldn't help wondering if Cal wasn't already too late. If Reese was somewhere close by, waiting to strike.

She could hear little Tiffany in the kitchen humming and water splashing. To Fiona she said, "I know we'll have to wash and sterilize those bottles again, but it was the only thing I could think of to keep her busy."

"You're a genius. Don't worry about it."

Dialing Zane's number again, Abby walked to the window and stood to the side, glancing out. Last time she'd talked to him, he'd been in the barn, checking the horses.

Again, she didn't get an answer. Turning back to Fiona, she said, "I'm worried. When Cal called, he said he'd found Reese's car and was going after him."

Fiona frowned at her. "So everything should be fine. Right?"

"Should be."

"Then what's to worry about?"

"I can't get his words out of my head. You didn't see the expression on his face, you don't understand—" She stopped her whispered words. Abby could see the curiosity on Fiona's face and knew the woman was wondering exactly what Abby had done to earn such animosity from Keira's husband. But that was one thing Abby wasn't going to share with Fiona. At least not until after her baby was here safe and sound.

"Abby—"

Cutting her off, Abby said, "I'm going down to the barn to see if Zane's okay. I'm really worried that he hasn't called me back or come up to the house. I'll be right back."

Fiona's brows rose and fear stood out in her eyes. "No. You can't leave."

She heard Fiona begin another contraction. Spinning,

she went to the woman who insisted on sitting in the re- cliner. "Do you want to lie down?"

"No way. Can't breathe when I do."

Abby flinched. Keira had complained of that same thing.

And then Fiona couldn't say anything for the next several minutes.

The contraction passed and Abby looked at her. "Do you feel the urge to push yet?"

"No, not yet."

"Will you let me examine you?"

Fiona flushed. "Sure. You're a doctor, right?"

"Not only am I a doctor, but I deliver babies for a living."

"What?" the woman nearly screeched. Then let out a breathless laugh. "God is so funny. I can't believe He sent you at the perfect time. Then again, I suppose I can."

Abby helped Fiona to the bed in her room and propped her up with pillows behind her.

Then she got to the examination.

"Oh, boy," Abby breathed, "you won't be long. You're almost a ten."

Fiona groaned. "I thought I'd be at least a twelve by now."

Abby couldn't help the chuckle that escaped her. "At least you're keeping your sense of humor."

"Might as well."

After Abby washed her hands, she walked back to the window in the direction of the barn, contemplating whether she should take a chance on leaving the house. Leaving Fiona and Tiffany.

As Abby looked toward the barn, she noticed a hint of...smoke?

She stood straighter. Looked harder. Was that a flame coming from the top of the roof?

She waited, just watching.

The smoke blew thicker and she definitely saw flames.

Whirling, she grabbed Fiona's big coat. "I hate to tell you this, but I think the barn's on fire. I'm going to have to go look. Zane's not answering his phone and if there's a fire…with the horses… I promise, I'll come right back."

Alarmed, Fiona sat up. "On fire!"

Abby shushed her. "It may be nothing, but I'm going to check. You stay here." Thinking, she grabbed the portable handset, dialed a number and handed it to the woman. Within a second, Abby's cell phone vibrated in her pocket. "I have you on the line. If you think you need to push, you holler at me and I'll get back here as fast as I can, all right? Can you handle me leaving you with Tiffany for a few minutes?"

Looking like she wasn't sure about that at all, Fiona, nevertheless, nodded and Abby didn't waste any more time. She raced from the room, checked on Tiffany who was now drying the bottles, then out the back door and hit the snow hard. She slipped and fell. Gathered herself up and pushed her way through the snow toward the barn desperately wishing Cal was here.

Finally, she made it to the door of the barn. Heart thudding, blood humming, she could hear the horses' frantic cries.

She placed her hand on the door. Cool. But the smoke was thick, swirling around her, seeping out through the cracks. "Zane!"

"Abby! Are you okay? What's happening?" Fiona's frightened cry came through the speaker on the phone.

Abby threw open the barn door and flinched as the smoke rolled out. "I'm fine," she hollered into the phone. "I'm going into the barn to let the horses out and pray Zane's not trapped in here somewhere." Coughing, she waited until the worst of the smoke billowed out. "Zane! Where are you?"

No answer.

"Abby! I need you!" Fiona cried.

Abby froze.

Her sister's pleading. "Abby, I need you to do this for me. You're the one I trust. Don't let me down."

Blinking against a rush of tears she didn't have time to shed, Abby said into the phone. "Call Cal. Tell him he's just going to have to let Reese go for now. Tell him you need him here!"

Fiona didn't answer.

Abby entered the barn and started opening stalls. "Hee-ya! Come on! Go!" She herded them toward the back entrance that opened into a pasture. Horse after horse rushed out. Smoke choked her. Then her foot caught on something and she fell hard. Gasping, working blind in the smoke, she used her hands to guide her.

And found—a body.

FIFTEEN

Cal tracked the blood and the steps in the snow. The physical exertion kept him warm. Worry and determination ran hot through his veins. If Reese Kirkpatrick was on this property, Cal would find him.

As he tracked, he prayed. For Fiona, for Zane—why wasn't the man answering his phone?—for Joseph. And for Abby.

And he couldn't think about Abby without remembering that incredible kiss in the kitchen. It seared his mind and made him long for more.

He ground his teeth. He needed to get back to the house. His sister was in labor, Abby had a killer after her and Zane wasn't answering his phone.

Things were not looking good as the blood trail led toward the house.

Cal stumbled, went to his knees.

Found more blood. Two feet later, he found the man it had come from. "Aw, no. Don't be dead," Cal whispered. He wanted some answers.

"Dying would be too easy for you. I want you alive, you jerk. Do you know what you've put us through?" He kept up a muttered monologue as it helped him think.

Using his teeth, he pulled off a glove and placed his fingers against the man's neck.

A steady pulse and Cal sighed in relief. And at least Reese was dressed appropriately for the weather. He wouldn't freeze to death. Yet. Cal couldn't see any sign of blood on his back.

With a grunt, Cal shoved his glove back on, then grasped the man under his arms and rolled him over.

A frown pulled Cal's brows together as his brain processed the information his eyes took in.

Reese had been shot in the upper part of his shoulder.

As he made the diagnosis, a groan came from the wounded man's lips. Cal reached for his cell phone.

Eli answered on the second ring. "Hello?"

"I found him."

"You got everything under control?"

"Not really. He's been shot and needs a hospital."

"Shot!" Eli exclaimed. "You shoot him?"

"Nope."

"Where's the shooter?"

Cal looked around the property. White as far as the eye could see. "I don't know, Eli, but this makes me really nervous."

Eli grunted. "If Reese is the one after Abby, why is he the one getting shot?"

"As soon as he comes to, I plan to ask him." Another groan from Reese. He was waking up. Good. Maybe now he'd get some answers.

Eli asked, "Did Joel make it out there?"

"Haven't heard from him and Zane's not answering his phone."

Cal heard Eli bite off a word he'd quit saying a long time ago. Cal said, "Fiona's in labor. I've got to get back to the house."

"Abby," the wounded man whispered.

"Hang on, Eli, he's trying to say something." He leaned over Reese. "What is it, man? Talk to me."

Reese's eyes fluttered. "Abby...danger."

"Yeah, she was in danger, but not anymore." Maybe, depending on whether Reese was telling the truth. "I got you."

"No, she's...gotta help her."

"I am helping her. Why are you after her?"

"Not..."

The man's eyes closed as he passed out once again.

Cal looked toward Fiona's house. And frowned. Was that smoke reaching for the sky?

"Cal? You there?"

"Yeah. Something weird is going on. Reese just passed out, but sounded like he was trying to say he wanted to help Abby." He narrowed his eyes. "And I'm seeing smoke in the direction of my sister's house."

Eli sighed. "I'll see if I can get a hold of Joel and get a location on him."

"I've got to call the house. Let me know what you find out." Hanging up on Eli, Cal then dialed the house number.

No answer.

He dialed Zane.

No answer.

Not liking the feeling in his gut, he hauled the wounded man up with a grunt and slung him over his back. Slowly, he began the trek back to the vehicles. He hoped he wasn't making things worse with the injury, but he sure couldn't leave the guy in the snow. Calling an ambulance would be fruitless. If it couldn't get to Fiona, it couldn't get to Reese.

Another glance toward Fiona and Joseph's house

tightened his midsection. No one answering the phones and smoke? He had a feeling that was a really bad combination and that the man he'd just found wasn't the enemy.

And that the enemy was already making his move.

Heart thudding, Abby felt for a pulse. "Zane? Oh please, don't be dead."

Her lungs felt like they were on fire and she knew she had to get out of the barn or she would pass out and die of smoke inhalation.

But she couldn't leave Zane.

And she couldn't pull him out of the barn.

She went face down on the floor and was able to gasp in a relatively smoke-free breath.

Darting to the watering trough, she pulled her scarf from around her neck and dunked it in the water. Wrapping it around her nose and mouth, she shuddered when the cold water touched her skin.

Nevertheless, she didn't stop. The horses still trapped whinnied and pawed the ground. Their frantic cries wrenched her heart. The protective barrier of the wet scarf helped and she went from stall to stall letting them out. At the last stall, she, grabbed the halter from the wall and got it over the last horse's head.

He bobbed and tried to dance past her to reach the door but Abby held on tight. Next, she threw a saddle on him and tightened the cinch.

Abby led the horse to Zane and working as fast as possible, she tied a rope around the man's chest careful to leave it long enough so he wouldn't get kicked by the horse.

Attaching the rope to the saddle horn, she grabbed the halter and tugged the horse toward the door. Anxious to escape the smoky barn, the animal didn't need much tugging. Abby kept her hand on the halter so that the horse wouldn't go too far with Zane attached to him.

Finally outside and several yards from the barn, she pulled in a lungful of fresh air and yanked the horse to an uneasy stop.

Shaking fingers fumbled with the rope and somehow she managed to free Zane from the horse. Dropping next to the man she checked Zane's breathing. His chest rose and fell. Fortunately for him, he'd fallen almost face-down where he'd breathed the cleaner air at the floor and not the smoky air swirling up above him. Next she checked him for any other wounds and found a lump on his head.

Her fingers probed the area even as her mind clicked through various scenarios as to what could have happened.

A loud crash sounded behind her. She flinched and whirled. A portion of the barn must have caved in.

"Abby! Abby! Are you there?"

Abby snatched the phone she'd left on speaker phone and pressed it to her ear. "I'm here, Fiona. I found Zane. He's alive but unconscious. Let me see if I can wake him up. There's no way I can carry him. I'll be there as soon as I can get Zane on his feet."

Torn, Abby stared down at Zane, wondering how she was going to get the man back up to the house.

"Hello, Abby."

Abby froze. Blinked.

Then spun. Surprise and shock rippled through her. "So, it was you all the time."

Cal lugged Reese back to the snowmobile and then realized there was no way he was going to be able to keep Reese on the machine and drive it safely back to his house.

Concerned, wondering exactly how much blood the man had lost, Cal turned his attention toward the SUV. Balancing Reese with one arm, he used the other to open the back door. As carefully as possible, he settled Reese into the backseat. Reese groaned and came to for the second time. "Where is she? Where's Abby? Gotta talk to her. Got to tell her—" His words slurred and his eyes rolled back.

Cal ignored him and climbed into the driver's seat. There was no way this man was getting anywhere near Abby until he was a hundred-percent sure he wasn't a threat to the woman he loved.

Shock rippled through him at his self-admission, but he realized it was true. He did love her and was anxious to get back and make sure she was all right.

Again, as he looked in the direction of home, the rising column of smoke shot fear through him. Reaching for his cell, he noticed he'd missed about four calls.

Speed dialing Fiona, he cranked the car.

Then groaned when the engine sputtered and died.

Abby stared at the man in front of her. He was the one who'd set her up.

Not Reese.

"Abby! I need you!" Fiona's voice came through the phone. Spinning, she ignored the danger behind her and raced for the house as fast as she could go through the thick snow. Then she faltered, stumbled.

He caught her by the arm and jerked her so hard that she nearly fell back to the ground. Pain shot up her arm as he demanded, "Where is it?"

"Where is what?" She wiped the snow from her face and shivered with cold and fear.

"The flash drive. Lisa saw you copying stuff on it. And when you disappeared she was worried what you might have taken with you. I did a little investigating. Looks like she was right to be worried."

Randall Cromwell's fingers dug into her arm and she winced. Staring up into her partner's face, she tried to jerk out of his grip. "Let me go."

He held tight. "After I get the flash drive."

Abby gritted her teeth as terror shot through her. He had no intention of letting her go. He couldn't. She swallowed hard. "That's what you were looking for? That's why you've been after me? I can't believe I didn't see through you. Well, that flash drive is in a safe place. You'll never get it," she taunted him.

His hand came around and clipped her in the side of the head. Stunned, she gave a hoarse cry and dropped to her knees.

He jerked her back up.

Fiona's desperate cry through the phone reached her once again.

"Who is that?" Randall demanded. "That pregnant woman?"

Fury lent her strength and determination. "Yes," she spat. "And she needs me to deliver her baby."

In desperation, Abby brought her fist around in a lightning fast move and slammed it into Randall's nose.

His harsh scream of pain sent bolts of satisfaction through her as she spun out of his loosened grasp. Shock almost held her immobile. She couldn't believe she'd actually managed to punch someone. Then she shoved the shock away and scuttled backward ignoring her throbbing hand, hoping she hadn't broken anything.

She needed to focus on escaping and getting to the house. Ignoring Randall's cries of pain and fury, ignoring the pain in her head from his blow, Abby channeled her energy into getting back to the house.

"Abby, please! I need you!"

She followed her previous tracks back to the house as fast as she could go. She could hear Randall cursing her and coming after her.

Breathless, lungs straining, she finally reached the front door and slammed her fist on it. "Fiona! Tiffany! Open the door!" Could the woman even walk at this point? Would the child be able to work the dead bolt?

A glance over her shoulder showed Randall gaining on her. Blood from his nose splattered the ground with each step he took. Pure fury radiated from him and she shivered. "Fiona!"

The door swung inward and Abby almost fell inside as she twisted to slam the door behind her. She clicked the dead bolts home and turned to find Fiona bent double making her way back to the bedroom. Tiffany stood in the door to the kitchen staring with wide eyes. "I finished the bottles," she said.

"Thank you, sweetheart," Abby managed to gasp. "You did a good job, I'm sure."

"What can I do now?" the little girl wanted to know.

Doing her best to stay calm, Abby said, "You can go in the bedroom and watch a video for a little while, okay?"

"I don't want to."

"Please, darling."

Where was help?

Terror seized her by the throat and wouldn't let go. She grabbed the phone to call Cal.

And listened to dead silence.

Then the lights went out.

Cal grunted as he slammed the hood on the car and climbed back into the driver's seat.

"Abby," the man in the back whispered again.

A file sat in the passenger side.

"He's going to kill her."

Cal barely caught the sentence. He turned and stared into Reese's bleary eyes. "Who?"

Reese licked his lips and Cal grabbed the open bottle of water from the cup holder and twisted to offer it to the man. Reese drank greedily, then pushed it away.

"What happened to you?" Cal demanded.

"I got ambushed," he grunted. "I've been trying to get to Abby for two weeks now. But she's got a restraining order out on me, so I've had to be careful. Then I lost her when she took off. I've been tracking her down ever since." He took another swig of water. "I've been in contact with my partner in Washington who's been looking into Abby's medical practice." Shame washed over Reese's face and Cal wondered at it. "I've been looking for a way to discredit her and thought I'd found it. False insurance reports."

"Wait a minute, I talked to your partner. He never said anything about y'all investigating Abby, just that you were completely unglued about your wife's death."

Reese grimaced. "Which was the truth, just not all of it. I asked him not to let on about what I was looking for. I convinced him that I knew Abby didn't deserve to be practicing medicine, I just needed to find the proof so I could shut her down. I asked him to tell that story if anyone started asking where I was." He groaned and closed his eyes. "Sure couldn't let people know I was violating a restraining order."

"Why would you?"

Reese swallowed hard and didn't answer. Cal wondered if the man had passed out again. Then Reese roused a bit to say, "Because after putting two and two together, I got the impression that Abby was in trouble. She thought it was me, I knew it wasn't."

"Abby wouldn't be involved in that kind of thing," Cal ground out. "She's found the insurance fraud, too. Someone set her up."

Reese hitched a breath and nodded. "I know. Look, I'll explain everything later. We need to get to Abby. That guy, Randall, is the one who shot me. He's also the one who's been stealing the money and making it look like it's Abby."

Cal tried the car again and was rewarded with a coughing growl. But at least it started. He'd have to get Zane to bring him back and get the snowmobile, but that was the least of his worries right now.

"How bad are you hit?" he asked Reese.

"Nothing major, obviously," Reese muttered. "I'm still here."

Cal studied the guy in the rearview mirror wondering if his story was on the up and up. He was inclined to believe it wasn't, that it was all a setup to get to Abby. But if it was... "And the guy who shot you is on the way to the house right now?"

"Yeah."

"Then hang on, that's where we're going, too."

Cal spun the wheel and waited for the chains on the tires to grip into the snow. Then he made his way as fast as possible, searching for the driveway. Reese hadn't known the layout of the land and he'd been driving across the field.

He was lucky he hadn't landed in a ditch somewhere. Even with the snow covering the ground, Cal knew where to drive and what area to avoid. At least the majority of them. The only problem was the ice and snow.

It was slow-going, but as long as the engine didn't die again, he'd be at the house within ten minutes.

Hang on, Abby, I'm coming.

Abby glanced out the window and sucked in a deep breath. Randall had made an icepack out of the snow and one of his gloves and held it on his nose. Every so often, he threw a menacing glance toward the house.

The barn continued to burn, but there wasn't anything Abby could do about it now. Leaving Zane worried her, but she'd had no choice. She had to take care of Fiona.

With no power, the house rapidly chilled. With a new baby on the way, she needed warmth. Abby cranked up the gas logs and prayed that would warm at least the den area.

Checking her cell phone, she prayed she could get one call out to Cal before it died. Dialing the number, she waited.

He answered with a snapped question. "Abby, are you all right?"

"No. Zane's unconscious out by the barn and Randall Cromwell, my partner, is here and trying to—"

The line cut off and she brought the phone down in front of her to look at it.

Dead. Like she would be if she didn't figure out something fast.

And Abby worried about Zane. She had to find a way to get back out there to check on him.

Fiona let out a keening cry from the bedroom and Abby raced to help. Tiffany bolted out of the spare room where she'd been playing with a flashlight Abby had managed to grab from the kitchen counter, and into the hall, eyes wide. "What's wrong with Aunt Fiona?"

"She's not feeling too well right now. But she'll be just fine in a bit. I'm going to take care of her, okay?"

Worried gray eyes stared at her. "Okay."

"There's nothing to worry about, I promise." Abby wondered if she wasn't trying to reassure herself as well as the little girl.

Abby paused. She didn't want to frighten Tiffany, but she spun back and said, "Sweetie, there's a bad man around the house. I want you to go hide if you see a man you don't know, okay?"

Tiffany frowned. "A bad man?"

"Yes. And if you see him, you hide. Promise?"

Tiffany nodded slowly, her little mind processing this. "Okay. I promise."

Her lower lip trembled, and Abby pulled her into a reassuring hug. She had to keep her safe. Had to help Fiona. Fear shuddered through her, but she pushed it away.

With one last pat on Tiffany's back, Abby said, "I need to check on Aunt Fiona now, all right?"

Tiffany went back to her video and Abby hurried to Fiona.

It wouldn't be long before Randall tried to get into the house. She knew this in her gut.

But she had a baby to deliver. If Randall got in, she'd just have to deal with that when the time came.

Please, God, I know I haven't prayed much since

*Keira died, but I really need You right now. And so does
Zane. Please watch over him until I can get back out
there. And please, please, get Cal here in time to stop
Randall.*

She found Fiona in the throes of another contraction.

After it passed, Abby quickly checked the woman
and told her. "Time to push."

SIXTEEN

Cal glanced in the rearview mirror once more. Reese had passed out again. But Cal was getting closer to the house. On the phone with Eli, he asked, "Anyone at Fiona's house yet?"

"No, Cal, I'm sorry. Joel hasn't reported in yet. To tell you the truth, I'm worried about him. This isn't like him."

Cal felt his stomach clench. "So am I. Abby just called and said Randall was at the house, then her phone died. I'm going to need backup."

"I figured. I'm on the way."

The snow swirled and he could barely see out of the windshield. "It's getting worse out here. Use a snow-mobile."

"Got it covered."

Cal hung up and tried Fiona again. Nothing.

Then the SUV slammed to the right, the steering wheel spun from his grip and the vehicle tilted. He'd hit a ditch or blown a tire.

Heart pounding with the adrenaline rush, he tried backing up, then going forward. Nothing worked.

Frustration made him want to let out a yell. Instead, he slammed a fist on the wheel and kicked the door open. Climbing out into the cold, he shivered and pulled his hat farther over his ears. He walked around to the other side and looked at the tires.

One was shredded.

Opening the passenger door, he shook the unconscious man. "Hey, Reese. Wake up."

Reese groaned, but didn't open his eyes.

Cal said, "I gotta leave you here, but I'll be back."

"Abby…"

"Yeah." He said a prayer for the man, slammed the door and started the difficult trek through the knee-deep snow toward the house he knew he'd be able to see just over the next rise.

Abby ran the warm washcloth over the baby boy in her arms as Fiona took a moment to gather her strength. She looked at the new mother. "I think that's the fastest first birth I've ever seen." Well, not really. Fiona had been in labor for days, they'd just both been in denial about the fact. Each one for different reasons, but denial all the same.

And now he was here.

The newborn let out a squall that made Abby sigh in relief. He sounded healthy—and mad. That was a good sign. Fiona looked fine. Radiant. And happy it was all over. Abby felt exhausted, mentally and physically. And so happy that everything went well with the birth, she wanted to weep.

But she didn't have time for that. Down the hall, she heard the sound of glass breaking.

Randall looking for a way in. Tensing, she handed the baby to Fiona who looked at Abby. "What was that?"

She couldn't lie, couldn't gloss over it. "It's the man who's been after me."

Fiona's eyes widened as fear entered them. "How do you know?"

"He was at the barn. He was the one who set it on fire."

"Zane! Is he all right?"

Abby winced. "I don't know. He was hurt when I left him. I need to find a way to check on him, but I…" Abby stopped and thought, trying to develop a plan.

Fiona shook her head. "You can't go out there, not with that man here. Just wait. You got in touch with Cal. He knows something's wrong and will be doing his best to get back here."

That statement brought a measure of hope; however, she still didn't know how bad Zane was hurt. The man had done his best to help keep her safe.

She could do no less for him. And if she stayed in the house, she might very well put Fiona, Tiffany and the baby in danger.

She thought quickly. "I'm going to get Tiffany and you keep her in here with you."

Abby stepped out of the bedroom, pushed down her mounting fear and crossed the hall where Tiffany still played with the flashlight. "Come with me, hon. I need you to come see the new baby."

Tiffany hopped up, the flashlight in hand. "New baby? Where? I wanna see."

Abby glanced down the hall and into the kitchen. So far, she could see nothing, but she wasn't sure which window Randall had broken and how fast he could gain access, but she knew it wouldn't be long.

She reentered Fiona's master bedroom and watched Tiffany climb up on the bed to see the baby. She caught Fiona's fearful gaze with her own and said, "I'll be right back."

Stepping back into the hall, she locked the bedroom door from the inside, and walked down the hall toward the sounds coming from the den. "Abby!" Randall hollered at her. "Where are you?"

Abby shuddered at the sheer menace in the man's tone. So, he was inside now. She stepped quietly, her shoes making no noise on the carpet runner. She needed a weapon. Somehow she had to keep Randall from going down the hall to check the bedrooms. As soon as he found the locked door, he'd break it down.

Indecision raged inside of her. What should she do? *Oh, Cal, where are you? I need you to hurry up!*

If Abby returned to the room where Fiona was, she'd have to knock and make noise.

Better to just try and find a way to knock Randall out before he got to Fiona's room.

But what could she use?

He had the kitchen blocked, but if he walked down the steps to the little apartment, she could slip into the kitchen.

Or she could make a run for the front door. Lead him away from the house and back toward the barn.

But no. Zane was there and injured. Randall could use him to get Abby to do whatever he wanted. So she'd have to aim for the main house.

Heart pounding, lungs desperately wanting to gasp air, she continued to the end of the hall. She could hear Randall opening and closing doors.

Light from the big windows in the den and the kitchen made it easy to see. Finally, Randall turned his back and she slipped into the den to crouch behind the large recliner. As soon as he got far enough away from the kitchen and the front door, she'd make a run for it.

Randall's vicious curses rang through her ears and she pressed her lips together to breathe through her nose.

Footsteps came her way.

She closed her eyes and prayed. *Please go the other way, please—*

Only to have that prayer interrupted by the feel of a gun against the back of her head.

Cal's anxiety level had already reached new highs. His breath labored in his lungs as he fought the snow and ice to get to Fiona's house. He estimated he was about another quarter of a mile away.

Grabbing his cell phone, he punched in Eli's number once again. The man answered on the second ring. "What is it?"

"Where are you?"

"Right at the edge of your property. About two miles out. Where are you?"

Panting, Cal said, "On foot. The car broke down on me. Flat tire. But I'm almost there. Had to leave Reese in the car."

"I'm coming as fast as I can, but it's slow-going."

"I know. Be careful. But hurry. Anything from Joel?"

"No."

Cal could hear the worry in his friend's voice. Finally, the house came in to view.

And the barn.

He came to a stumbling halt, shock rendering him nearly motionless. "Oh, my—"

"What is it? What's wrong?"

Eli's question cracked across him and fear tumbled headlong through his heart.

"The barn's on fire. It looks like a total loss."

With renewed adrenaline shooting through him, Cal

picked up the pace. His prayers winged Heavenward.
Please, Lord...

He could see the horses in the far pasture. It looked
like someone had managed to get them out. But as valu-
able as the horses were, his main concern was Abby,
Fiona, Tiffany and Zane.

He could also see a snowmobile parked to the left
side of the house.

Cromwell.

Pushing himself to the limit, he raced through the
constricting snow, desperately praying he wasn't too
late.

Abby froze wondering what had given her away.

"Stand up." The low order scraped over her skin.

Slowly, she rose from her crouched position behind
the chair, turned and saw the mirror on the wall, expos-
ing her hiding place. Her heart thudded against her chest
and her breathing seemed constricted. Fear thrummed
a steady beat through her veins and she kept a tight rein
on her nerves.

Cal, where are you?

But this was her fault. She'd brought this trouble into
the McIvers' household, it was up to her to get rid of it.

One way or another.

The gun dug into the back of her skull and she
winced.

"Get me the flash drive. Now," Randall ordered. His
cold calculated words made her shiver.

Abby wanted to stall. She needed time to think. Because once she gave him what he wanted, he'd have no
reason to keep her alive.

Randall pulled the gun from her head and spun her
by the shoulder to face him. When she looked into his

eyes, her terror tripled. She'd never stared evil in the face before. But she knew she was looking at it now.

And she knew her time had run out.

"Fine. Okay. You win."

Even as she said the word, a plan formed in the back of her mind.

And the baby cried.

Randall's eyes cut to the hall, then back to her. "And no tricks or I'll kill both of them."

Abby shuddered. And knew she didn't have a choice any longer. "Follow me. I'm staying down in the basement." She didn't worry that he would think she was lying. After all, that's where he'd tried his first attempt to nab her. There was no way he could know that she'd moved upstairs. "The drive's down there in my purse."

A wary look replaced the meanness. "Then you go down first."

She nodded, walked into the kitchen and started down the steps. The darkness pressed in on her. Not having any light in the stairwell, she held on to the rail to help guide her. One by one, she took the steps, descending to the basement on shaky legs. Two steps from the bottom, she opened the door and took a deep breath.

Prayed for strength and courage to do the right thing.

"What are you waiting for?" The muzzle of the gun nudged her forward.

Courage, she thought. *Lord, please help me.*

Taking in another bolstering breath, she forced herself not give in to the fear…or to chicken out on doing what she knew she had to do.

She'd only have a split second to act.

Fortunately, outside light filtered through the window, illuminating her way. Giving her just enough light to see what she needed to see.

Heart thumping, stomach churning, she reached the last step, spun out of sight around the edge of the wall that hid the steps—and Randall's view—and grabbed the nearest rifle from the display rack.

"Hey! What are you—" He came around the corner, his blackened eyes widening in the fraction of the second he realized her intention.

Swinging the rifle by the barrel, she slammed the butt of the weapon into Randall's already-broken nose.

His screeching cry of pain echoed around her as she bolted past him. His hand shot out and snagged her leg. Hard fingers dug into her as he pulled her foot out from under her. She landed on the steps with bone-jarring thud.

"Let go of me!"

Abby scrambled to claw her way up, but Randall just wouldn't loosen his grip. She kicked out with her free leg and caught him under the chin.

He gave another howl and she was free.

Knowing she was dead if he got his hands on her again, she crawled on all fours up the stairs, slid through the open door at the top and slammed it behind her.

Shooting to her feet, she rammed the lock home, then searched for another weapon, her breath hitching in her chest, hands shaking. Now he would be extra mad and would probably just shoot her on sight. And everyone else he came in contact with.

Somehow she had to get him out of the house.

She opened cabinets, then shut them, seeing nothing that would be useful. Eyeing the block of knives on the counter, she gulped. Would she be able to use one in a way that meant possibly killing Randall?

She thought about Fiona, the baby and Tiffany.

Maybe.

She stopped. Randall was in the basement. If she could get Abby, the baby and Tiffany out of the house…

But that would be impossible. No, she had to take care of Randall. One way or another.

An open drawer revealed a silver roll of duct tape. She snatched it and placed it on the counter. If she could knock Randall out, she could use the duct tape to keep him in one place until help could arrive.

Shaking, she started looking for a heavy frying pan.

A noise at the front door startled her and she raced over to look out the window.

Had Randall gone out the basement door and come around to the front?

Pushing aside the curtain, Abby looked out and nearly wilted with relief. She unlocked the dead bolt and threw the door open. "Cal!"

"Are you okay?" He grabbed her and looked past her. "Is Fiona all right?"

"Yes, but Randall's here. He's in the basement and—"

"I'm going to kill you!" Randall's enraged scream came from behind the locked door and echoed throughout the house.

Cal had his weapon ready in less than a second while he pushed Abby toward the hall. "Get in one of the bedrooms and lock the door."

"Abby!" Fiona's scared shout distracted her. Then the baby cried.

Cal looked startled but didn't have time to question her as a loud crash sounded from the kitchen. "He's trying to break down the door," she whispered.

"Go! Down the hall. Now. He doesn't know I'm here. I'm going to use that to our advantage."

Tension and determination lined Cal's face as Abby

hung back, not wanting to get in the way, but unwilling to cower in a bedroom behind a closed door while Cal faced down a man she'd brought into his life. Cal slid into the kitchen and positioned himself just to the side of the door that led down to the basement.

Another crash rattled it.

Cal reached up and unlocked it, then readied himself for the next blow.

Abby's eyes darted for a weapon and landed on a heavy brass lamp.

Another crash sent the door slamming into the wall and Randall's bloody, bruised face appeared. His eyes landed on hers and took one step toward her.

Cal settled his weapon against the side of the man's head and said, "Drop the gun."

Randall froze.

Then exploded.

With a crazed yell, he spun, taking Cal by surprise. Randall's gun went off and the bullet slammed into the opposite wall.

Abby wanted to add her screams of terror to the commotion, but her paralyzed throat wouldn't make a sound. She thought she heard Tiffany crying from down the hall.

Cal's gun hit the floor, skidding across the hardwood as Randall tried to bring his weapon around to point it at Cal.

Breaking free from her stunned frozen state, Abby snatched the brass lamp from the stand in the foyer and slinked toward the two struggling men.

On shaky legs, she moved closer, finger cramped around the lamp. Cal had Randall on the floor, his fingers gripped around the man's wrist, pushing the gun from aiming in his direction.

Praying, tears leaking in spite of her best efforts to hold them back, she lifted the lamp.

Waited.

Cal grunted, shoved the gun from his face.

Abby breathed in.

And waited.

And then Cal gave her the opening she needed. He rolled to the side presenting Randall's back to her. She brought the lamp down.

Randall moved, messing up the blow she'd intended for the back of his head but she caught him just above the ear. It worked just as well.

He went down and was still, bleeding from his wounds, but still breathing from what she could tell.

Cal ripped the gun from the man's limp fingers, flipped him on his stomach and slapped handcuffs on his wrists.

Then Cal sat back and took a deep breath.

Abby walked over and sank to the floor beside him.

He wrapped his arm around her shoulders and pulled her to him.

Head resting on his chest, she said, "I love you."

Cal's insides shivered at the sweet words still ringing in his ears. Just as he was about to respond a knock at the door jolted them.

Cal helped Abby to her feet, placed a kiss on her lips, then went to open the door.

He heard Abby gasp as Reese Kirkpatrick stumbled into the foyer. Grasping the man by the arm, he said, "How'd you get here?"

"Walked."

"What happened to him?" Abby asked.

Cal led Reese to the couch and let the man lay back. Reese groaned and Cal said, "Randall shot him."

"What?" Abby blinked in disbelief as her gaze bounced back and forth between the men.

"Reese was on his way to warn you that he'd found evidence about your partner framing you to take the fall for the false insurance claims. Only Reese found Cromwell first and when confronted, Cromwell shot him and left him for dead."

"Cromwell sent that note, by the way," Reese said. "After he shot me, he took great pleasure in telling me how you blamed me for everything he was doing."

Abby grimaced. "Wish you would have called me."

"Couldn't call you or approach you without scaring you to death," Reese whispered. "And violating that restraining order."

Abby winced. Worried green eyes met Cal's. "You need to check on Zane. He was out cold by the barn when I had to run from Randall." She shot a glare in the direction of the unconscious man, then returned to check on Reese.

The lights flickered. Then came on. Cal breathed a sigh of relief. That was one thing he wouldn't have to worry about. He'd thought maybe Randall cut the line, but apparently the storm was the culprit.

Cal said, "Zane was trying to get up here to the house to help when I came across him. I sent him back to the bunkhouse. He's got a migraine, and bad case of vertigo and smoke inhalation, but he'll be all right." He glanced at his watch and felt his nerves clench. "I also called the EMS and told them to get through if they could." He strode to the window and looked out. "I'm guessing they can't."

Relief at his news about Zane stood out on her pretty

face and his heart tumbled around in his chest as emotions swept over him. Then she asked, "Can you get me some scissors? I need to get that shirt off of him and check the wound."

Reese had his eyes closed once more, his head lolled to one side.

"Sure." He got her the scissors. Walking into the den, he handed them to Abby. When she reached up to take them, her fingers grazed his. Longing speared him and he hoped his eyes conveyed the promise he wanted to make to her. A promise that said they had a future to discuss.

She blinked and red tinged her cheeks.

He smiled. She got the message.

Cal saw her professional mode switch on as she cut the shirt from her brother-in-law to examine the wound.

When she probed the area, Reese stirred and came to. "Hey, that hurts."

Abby ignored him and said, "I thought you wanted to kill me."

"No." Shame crossed his haggard features. "I was digging into your medical practice looking for something, anything to discredit you, anything that would justify having your license taken away." He cleared his throat and swallowed. "I couldn't find anything. Except it looked like you were into false insurance claims."

Sweat broke out over the man's brow and Abby frowned. "You can tell me the rest later." She reached up to place a hand on his face. "You're feverish."

Reese grabbed her wrist and looked at her. "I've spent close to the past two weeks chasing you. I need to tell you now that I don't blame you for their deaths. Not anymore."

Abby gasped and Cal felt a sweet peace invade him.

She would be all right after Reese finished his story. Reese shifted, winced and said, "I had to have indisputable proof that you were doing something illegal, but the more I dug, the more I found. With the help of the department's computer geek, I was able to find that all of the false transactions were entered either on Cromwell's computer or his secretary's."

"Lisa Wilde."

Reese nodded and licked his lips. "They're in it together. I took my proof to the captain who agreed not to arrest her until I tracked down Cromwell."

"So that's why you were coming after me?"

"Yes. Only I had to be careful. If I violated that restraining order, I could go to jail." He shot her a sardonic look. "And that wasn't going to happen. But then the stakes changed and I realized you were in real danger. I called Eli and filled him in."

"A little late," Cal grunted.

Reese flushed, but Abby couldn't tell if it was from the fever or Cal's admonition. "I didn't realize Cromwell had followed her. I actually didn't know he was involved until a few days ago. And when it came to light, I didn't know where Abby had gone. I finally managed to track her down, but she did a good job hiding her trail."

"Not good enough, Randall managed to find me," Abby said.

"Randall was probably already watching you, waiting for a chance to grab you. He did the same thing you did and used cash for everything. Traveled under a different name, too."

Abby frowned. "Then how did you find me?"

"Tracked your cell phone from a call you made to your parents a couple of days ago."

"So you weren't at the bus station when I thought I saw you," she murmured.

"No, but Randall was."

"He followed me to the doctor's office and then out to the ranch," Cal said. "I suspected as much."

A moan came from the kitchen and Cal immediately spun in that direction. Crossing the den, he walked to where he'd left Randall handcuffed on the floor.

The man looked bad. Pride rose up in him. Abby had defended herself well.

He reached down to grab Randall by the arm and hauled him to his feet. Randall cringed and Cal thought he looked like he might pass back out, but he didn't.

Randall just stood and hung his head pulling in deep breaths. Then he said, "Could I see a doctor? Please?"

"In a bit of pain, are you?"

"You might say that." The words came through gritted teeth. Cal almost felt sorry for the pain the man had to be in. Almost. "Yeah, we'll let you see a doctor as soon as we have access to one."

Cal walked Randall to the table and stuffed him into a kitchen chair. "Stay there." He pulled his cell phone out and dialed Eli's number. "Where are you, man?"

"I made it. I'm standing on Fiona's front porch."

Opening the door, Cal let the sheriff in. Gesturing to Randall, Cal said to Eli, "He's all yours. Better late than never, I guess."

"What happened out here?" Eli asked.

Cal filled him in while Abby took care of Reese.

Then Eli's phone rang. He listened, then shot a look at Cal. After he hung up, he said, "That was Joel. Apparently Cromwell got to him, too. Joel just woke up after someone cracked him across the head as he was walking out to the snowmobile in the back parking lot.

Dragged Joel into the back alley and stole the snowmobile."

"Which he used to get here," Cal surmised.

"Which was probably the strange noise I heard but couldn't place," Abby said.

The door opened again. Cal felt surprise run through him when his mother, followed by Jesse, stepped inside.

"How's Fiona?" Mrs. McIvers immediately asked about.

"She's in her bedroom."

"No, I'm not. I'm right here."

Eli escorted Randall Cromwell from the house while everyone turned as one to see Fiona standing at the entrance to the den, holding her son.

Cal looked at Jesse. "How did—"

"Drove my truck as far as we could, then hopped on the snowmobile I had in the back."

"My mother? Hopped on a snowmobile?"

Jesse shrugged. "I offered to bring her home. She refused at first. I offered again and when I explained I could get back to my family in time for Christmas, she took me up on it." His lips pulled into a grin. "I think she's hooked. Said something about buying one for Christmas."

Cal shook his head, gave Jesse a hug and said, "I owe you."

"Gotta run. See you in a few days." He glanced at Fiona. "Tell her congratulations. I look forward to getting to know the little one soon."

And then Cal's breath caught in his throat as he watched his mother hold her grandchild for the first time. His nephew. "What's his name?"

Fiona looked up. "Joseph Jameson Whitley."

"Jameson?" Cal whispered.

"Yes. For dad. We'll call him James."

Cal had to swallow the lump in his throat. His father would be so proud and honored to have his first grandson named after him. "We need to get on Skype so Joseph can see his son."

Fiona let the tears fall. "I've been on the phone with him. He's upset he wasn't able to be here, but relieved we're all fine."

Tiffany pushed her way next to Fiona. "I got to hold him. He's tiny and no fun yet, but I'll teach him all kinds of stuff when he gets bigger."

Cal laughed. His gaze snagged Abby's and he smiled at the tears standing in her eyes.

Only this time the tears weren't of pain or fear.

Joy and peace stood out.

He walked over to her and wrapped his arms around her, pulling her into a tight hug. Her arms slid around his waist and she leaned into him.

He whispered in her ear, "You did good."

A shudder racked her. "I was terrified."

"Of helping my sister give birth or of Randall?"

"Both."

"Abby?"

Cal let her look around him to the man on the couch. Reese reached behind him and pulled out a folded file he'd stuffed in the back of his waistband. He gestured for Abby to approach him.

She did and Reese handed the file to her.

Cal could see her confusion.

Reese took a deep breath and said, "It's the autopsy report."

SEVENTEEN

Abby froze.

The file suddenly weighed a thousand pounds.

"It wasn't your fault. It wasn't anyone's fault." The man's voice cracked. He cleared his throat. "She would have died even in a hospital," he whispered. "She had an aneurysm. It ruptured and she was gone almost instantly."

Abby swallowed hard. "And the baby?"

Reese winced. "We'll never know for sure. The report was inconclusive. I tried to tell you outside your office that day, but I could tell you were scared of me."

"So many weird things had happened. I thought you were after me."

"I know. I read the restraining order and the police reports you filed. I knew it wasn't me, so I figured I'd do a little investigating. I was curious as to who else wanted to…ah…" He flushed.

"Right. Who else wanted to do me harm."

"Aw, Abby, I was crazy with grief. I didn't really want to hurt you, I just…"

"Needed someone to blame," she whispered. "I get it."

He reached out to take her hand. "I'm sorry."

She sighed and shook her head, grief for her lost sister and the baby nearly smothering her. But she said, "All's forgiven. Keira wouldn't want this bitterness between us."

Tears stood out in his eyes. "Yeah." Then he groaned and winced. "I don't feel so great."

"You need a doctor. Antibiotics and possibly surgery." She looked at Cal. "Where's the EMS crew?"

He'd been listening and blinked when she suddenly addressed him. "They must not have been able to get through."

"What about another helicopter?"

"I asked. The wind's pretty bad out there. They're watching the conditions. If they get a window, they'll get out here."

Minutes ticked by as Abby monitored Reese.

"Can I do anything to help?" Cal's mother asked. "Fiona's taken the baby and gone back to the bedroom to rest."

Abby shook her head. "No, I've done everything that I can do. Now it's just wait on EMS to get through and get Reese and probably Zane to the hospital."

Cal nodded. "All right. I'm going to go check on Zane and see where the helicopter is and if they think they'll be able to make the flight. I know an ambulance is doing its best to get through, but they're coming from thirty minutes away."

"I'll keep an eye on him." Mrs. McIvers settled herself in the recliner and picked up the remote. "And her. Come here, Tiffany, let's see if we can find something on television. Want to snuggle with me?"

The child grinned and climbed into the woman's lap.

"You'll make an awesome grandmother," Abby said.

Mrs. McIvers grinned. "I've been waiting a long time to prove it, too."

Abby rose. "I'll go with Cal to check on Zane." She looked at Cal. "You want to show me where he is?"

"Sure."

They shrugged into their heavy coats and Cal led the way to the bunkhouse. Abby lifted her head and looked at the sky. "It's not as windy."

"Yeah, I noticed. Maybe the helicopter can get over here before too much longer."

Cal opened the door to the bunkhouse and Abby moved quickly to Zane's side and sat beside him on the bed. She checked him over. "He's in a deep sleep. What did he take?"

Cal reached for a bottle of pills on the bedside table and handed them to her. "Probably these."

"For migraines."

"Yeah."

"He looks like he's breathing all right, but I'd feel better if he'd go to the hospital and get checked out, too."

Cal nodded. "He will." He grasped her hand and pulled her to her feet.

Startled, her eyes met his. "What?"

He pulled her into large living area. "I've been wanting to do something since I found you safe."

She blinked at him. "What's that?"

"This."

His lips covered hers and she melted into his embrace, welcoming his affection, his love. When he lifted his head, he said, "I hope you don't have any plans to go anywhere anytime soon."

"I...well...my practice. There's going to be a lot to deal with there."

"I'll help you with that."

"And my parents." She swallowed hard. "I really need to keep trying with them."

"I can help with that, too."

"So what exactly are you saying, Cal?" She couldn't help that the words came out in a whisper. Her throat didn't seem to want to work.

"I'm saying that from the moment you fell at my feet in the bus station, I've felt something special for you. I've gone through a whole range of emotions in the past two weeks where you're concerned. I want a chance to explore what's between us."

She felt a smile tremble on her lips as her heart leaped with joy. "I want that, too."

"Then will you consider delivering babies in this little town? I assure you, you'll stay busy." He grinned. "I'm guessing about nine months from the date of this snow storm you might have your hands full of deliveries."

Abby gasped a giggle at his joke and said, "That sounds like a lovely plan."

"Oh, but there is one problem." He frowned.

Abby grew serious. "What?"

"In addition to you, we'll need another obstetrician in town."

"Why's that?"

"Because—" he leaned closer "—who's going to deliver your babies?"

Her eyes went wide. "My babies?"

He shrugged. "Okay, our babies."

Abby narrowed her eyes even as the thought of having a family with Cal sent delicious shivers up her spine. "Well, if we're having babies, I sure hope you've got a wedding in mind."

Cal grinned. "I do."

"Okay." Abby grinned back. "I do, too, then."

As Cal took possession of her lips once again, the thump of helicopter blades reached their ears.

She laughed. "Perfect timing."

"Yep." He looked up. "Everything's going to be okay."

"Yes, it is," Abby breathed. "I believe that for the first time in a really long time."

He looked down at her. "I know it seems impossible in such a short time, but I love you, Abby O'Sullivan."

"You're right, it doesn't seem possible, but I love you, too."

Together, they ran through the snow to meet the occupants of the helicopter, then hand in hand, headed for the house.

Abby lifted her eyes to the Heavens. She felt tears spring up and gave silent thanks to her Father for taking something horrible and bringing about something wonderful. And bringing her back to Him.

For the first time in a long time, she couldn't wait to see what her future would hold.

Because she knew in that future, Cal would be holding her.

And their babies.

* * * * *

Dear Reader,

I do hope you enjoyed another visit to Rose Mountain, North Carolina. I've really fallen in love with the little town and wish it were an actual place! But it's not, so I visit through my stories. Cal and Abby had a rough time there, especially Abby, facing her fears and her past. And Cal had to decide if he could trust a woman unwilling to share everything with him. Secrets separate, secrets can hurt, but sharing them can sometimes bring healing and peace. Abby finally decided she could share her secrets with Cal and in the end, she found she'd made the right decision. Cal had earned that trust with his gently pushy way and Abby benefited from it in the end.

I pray that if you're struggling with something, some kind of fear, you'll trust someone, share with someone who can help point you in the right direction in overcoming that fear.

God bless,

Lynette Eason

Questions for Discussion

1. Abby was on the run from the man she thought wanted to harm her. She'd finally had enough and reached her breaking point. Do you have a breaking point? If so, what do you think that would be?

2. Cal and his mother didn't hesitate to take in Abby, a stranger, when she was sick and seemed to be in danger. Unfortunately, in this day and age, that seems to be a rare occurrence. What would you have done in Cal's place?

3. Cal's quiet faith got to Abby. She realized he and his family had suffered their own tragedies in the loss of his father to a heart attack and a cousin to murder. What do you think about Cal's faith? What do you think about Abby's?

4. Abby was so sure she knew who was after her. In the end, she was wrong. Were you surprised by the ending? If so, why? If not, why not?

5. What was your favorite scene? Why?

6. Who was your favorite character? Why?

7. Have you read the other books in the Rose Mountain series? If not, do you think you might like to read them? They are *Dark Obsession* (a novella in the *My Deadly Valentine* anthology) and *Agent Undercover*.

8. What do you think about Abby's parents? Do you think they'll soften toward her eventually?

9. Have you ever been trapped at home because of heavy snow? How did it make you feel? Frightened? Or was it kind of fun? (I'm sure this can depend on your circumstances.)

10. When it came right down to it, Abby "womaned up" and did what she had to do to help not only little Daniel Brody, but also Fiona. Has there been a time in your life where you've had to push aside your own fears to do something that had to be done?

11. What do you think about Abby being willing to give up her lucrative medical practice to move to Rose Mountain? She really didn't have to think twice. Would you give up something like that? Why or why not?

12. Why do you like to read Romantic Suspense books?

13. Cal's faith meant a lot to him and he wanted to share it with Abby. He wasn't afraid or ashamed to try to point her back toward God. Who was the last person you talked to about your faith? Was it easy or kind of hard?

14. Even after the letter arrived accusing Abby of being a murderer, Cal didn't stop believing in her. Why was his faith in her so strong? What would you have done? Kicked her out like Joseph? Or brought her back home?

15. What do you think of Cal's mother? Do you think she would be a good example to follow? Why or why not?

INSPIRATIONAL

Wholesome romances that touch the heart and soul.

COMING NEXT MONTH
AVAILABLE JANUARY 10, 2012

THE SECRET HEIRESS
Protection Specialists
Terri Reed

THE LAWMAN'S LEGACY
Fitzgerald Bay
Shirlee McCoy

ESCAPE FROM THE BADLANDS
Dana Mentink

STALKER IN THE SHADOWS
Camy Tang

LISCNM1211

REQUEST YOUR FREE BOOKS!

2 FREE RIVETING INSPIRATIONAL NOVELS
PLUS 2 FREE MYSTERY GIFTS

YES! Please send me 2 FREE Love Inspired® Suspense novels and my 2 FREE mystery gifts (gifts are worth about $10). After receiving them, if I don't wish to receive any more books, I can return the shipping statement marked "cancel". If I don't cancel, I will receive 4 brand-new novels every month and be billed just $4.49 per book in the U.S. or $4.99 per book in Canada. That's a saving of at least 22% off the cover price. It's quite a bargain! Shipping and handling is just 50¢ per book in the U.S. and 75¢ per book in Canada.* I understand that accepting the 2 free books and gifts places me under no obligation to buy anything. I can always return a shipment and cancel at any time. Even if I never buy another book, the two free books and gifts are mine to keep forever.

123/323 IDN FEHR

Name	(PLEASE PRINT)

Address	Apt. #

City	State/Prov.	Zip/Postal Code

Signature (if under 18, a parent or guardian must sign)

Mail to the **Reader Service:**
IN U.S.A.: P.O. Box 1867, Buffalo, NY 14240-1867
IN CANADA: P.O. Box 609, Fort Erie, Ontario L2A 5X3

Not valid for current subscribers to Love Inspired Suspense books.

**Are you a subscriber to Love Inspired Suspense
and want to receive the larger-print edition?
Call 1-800-873-8635 or visit www.ReaderService.com.**

* Terms and prices subject to change without notice. Prices do not include applicable taxes. Sales tax applicable in N.Y. Canadian residents will be charged applicable taxes. Offer not valid in Quebec. This offer is limited to one order per household. All orders subject to credit approval. Credit or debit balances in a customer's account(s) may be offset by any other outstanding balance owed by or to the customer. Please allow 4 to 6 weeks for delivery. Offer available while quantities last.

Your Privacy—The Reader Service is committed to protecting your privacy. Our Privacy Policy is available online at www.ReaderService.com or upon request from the Reader Service.

We make a portion of our mailing list available to reputable third parties that offer products we believe may interest you. If you prefer that we not exchange your name with third parties, or if you wish to clarify or modify your communication preferences, please visit us at www.ReaderService.com/consumerschoice or write to us at Reader Service Preference Service, P.O. Box 9062, Buffalo, NY 14269. Include your complete name and address.

LISUS11B

*In the exciting new FITZGERALD BAY series
from Love Inspired Suspense, law enforcement siblings
fight for justice and family when one of their own
is accused of murder.*

*Read on for a sneak preview of the first book,
THE LAWMAN'S LEGACY by Shirlee McCoy.*

Police captain Douglas Fitzgerald stepped into his father's house. The entire Fitzgerald clan had gathered, and he was the last to arrive. Not a problem. He had a foolproof excuse. Duty first. That's the way his father had raised him. It was the only way he knew how to be.

Voices carried from the dining room. With his boisterous family around, his life could never be empty.

But there *were* moments when he felt that something was missing.

Some*one* was missing.

Before he could dwell on his thoughts, his radio crackled and the dispatcher came on.

"Captain? We have a situation on our hands. A body has been found near the lighthouse."

"Where?"

"At the base of the cliffs. The caller believes the deceased may be Olivia Henry."

"It can't be Olivia." Douglas's brother Charles spoke. The custodial parent to his twin toddlers, he employed Olivia as their nanny.

"I'll be there in ten minutes." He jogged back outside and jumped into his vehicle.

Douglas flew down Main Street and out onto the rural road that led to the bluff. Two police cars followed. His brothers and his father. Douglas was sure of it. Together, they'd piece together what had happened.

The lighthouse loomed in the distance, growing closer with every passing mile. A beat-up station wagon sat in the driveway.

Douglas got out and made his way along the path to the cliff.

Up ahead, a woman stood near the edge.

Meredith O'Leary.

There was no mistaking her strawberry-blond hair, her feminine curves, or the way his stomach clenched, his senses springing to life when he saw her.

"Merry!"

"Captain Fitzgerald! Olivia is…"

"Stay here. I'll take a look."

He approached the cliff's edge. Even from a distance, Douglas recognized the small frame.

His father stepped up beside him. "It's her."

"I'm afraid so."

"We need to be the first to examine the body. If she fell, fine. If she didn't, we need to know what happened."

If she fell.

The words seemed to hang in the air, the other possibilities hovering with them.

Can Merry work together with Douglas to find justice for Olivia…without giving up her own deadly secrets?
To find out, pick up
THE LAWMAN'S LEGACY by Shirlee McCoy,
on sale January 10, 2012.

SUSPENSE
RIVETING INSPIRATIONAL ROMANCE

FITZGERALD BAY

Law-enforcement siblings fight for justice and family.

Follow the men and women of Fitzgerald Bay as they unravel the mystery of their small town and find love in the process, with:

THE LAWMAN'S LEGACY by Shirlee McCoy
January 2012

THE ROOKIE'S ASSIGNMENT by Valerie Hansen
February 2012

THE DETECTIVE'S SECRET DAUGHTER
by Rachelle McCalla
March 2012

THE WIDOW'S PROTECTOR by Stephanie Newton
April 2012

THE BLACK SHEEP'S REDEMPTION by Lynette Eason
May 2012

THE DEPUTY'S DUTY by Terri Reed
June 2012

Available wherever books are sold.

www.LoveInspiredBooks.com

LISCONT12